BLOOD ON HIS HANDS

HENK MUNI

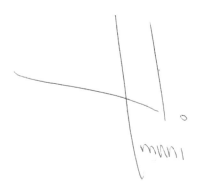

Blood on His Hands

1st Edition

Henk Muni

www.henkmuni.com

Copyright 2020 Henk Muni

Published by Henk Muni

ISBN (Paperback) 978-0-9959746-2-3

ISBN (Ebook) 978-0-9959746-3-0

Cover Design by Constance Mears

Layout by Stephanie Candiago

I dedicate this book to
the frontline workers fighting COVID-19

Blood on His Hands
By Henk Muni

1

Chris was amused by the blood clot dangling from his index finger and begging gravity to set it free. It finally let go and splattered on the hardwood, right beside the expanding pool of blood that quickly gobbled it up.

Thick, sticky blood covered Chris to the elbows. A strange metal stench filled the air as the warm passion for life that had previously occupied this home was replaced by the cold chill of death.

He watched the flow of blood ease to a stop.

"Stop to clot. Clot to scab. Scab to heal?" he mumbled to himself. "There is no healing this."

He closed his eyes.

"How did I get here? I am so fucked."

He opened his eyes in the hope of seeing a different scene, except nothing had changed. His neighbour's sleek, modern kitchen was covered in red. It was all over the white marble countertops, the neutral-coloured walls, and the beautiful hardwood floors.

"Look at this mess of red." He tilted his head slightly.

"It could be art," he said. "Weird, grim art that someone needs to explain to me."

He balled his hands into fists and then released them. The drying blood forced him to pry his fingers open.

He reached for his bloody cell phone on the kitchen counter. He wiped the screen against his pants until he could at least see part of it. The motion lit the phone and displayed the last-dialled number: 911.

They were on their way, although over the phone he had told them, "Don't rush. I think Sheldon's dead."

He'd tried the bit of CPR he'd learned from watching medical shows on TV, but shuddered at the noise Sheldon had made. "T should have been here instead. He's the one who always googles medical crap. He would've been way better than me," Chris mumbled as he tried to make sense of the inconceivable. "All I did was get blood all over me." He shuddered again as he recalled how Sheldon frothed and gurgled blood-spray out of his mouth and nose with every chest compression.

Chris stared at the knife. The scene appeared so foreign to him that Chris closed his eyes again, hoping to wake up from the nightmare. The blade was buried to the hilt; only the handle was visible, mounted between Sheldon's eyes. He wanted to pull it out, but the 911 operator had told him not to touch it, and he complied. "I guess it's too late anyway."

Sheldon was quiet now. Dead quiet.

Chris reached out and closed Sheldon's eyes to stop them from staring at the ceiling.

He looked north out the window, over the lake and toward the highway, knowing they'd be coming from there.

Then he saw the blue and red flashing lights. Police in front; ambulance in tow.

He looked down at his blood-soaked hands again, and a surge of panic rose in his stomach. "Oh my God, I am so screwed. They'll never believe I'm innocent. And if I'm not careful, they might even shoot me or something. The cops are crazy these days."

He walked to the kitchen sink, washed his hands, and wiped the blood off his face. He walked out the front entrance and sat down on the steps, leaving the front door open. As the red-and-blue dust cloud rose on the access road, he placed his hands on his head.

The convoy of police cars screeched to a halt in the driveway. Doors flew open, and police poured out, hollering commands.

The ambulance staff scurried past him up the steps, heading inside for the corpse of Dr. Sheldon Peterson.

Chris dropped his head between his knees.

2

Chris waited in the interrogation room. He was nervously looking about as he sat in the chair. It was a boring grey room with a table, a neon light, and a big mirror on the far side. The closed door had a small porthole window, and he could hear the activity in the police station beyond. Intermittently, there were whispers at the door and quick glances at him through the window. Whenever he made eye contact with an observer, they would immediately cast their eyes away and depart.

"I wonder how long this is going to take," he mumbled to himself. "No use asking for anything, I guess. I have been in here for hours." His knee was bouncing. He looked at the empty cup and, with a trembling hand, poured himself some more water from the plastic jug. He spilled some and chuckled to himself. "Wait here for questioning, they said, but not a single question yet. Who else are they talking to?"

He looked at his hands and was relieved he'd taken the time to wash them at the house, before they picked him up. He sniffed his armpit and recoiled at his own stench. The hot interrogation room made him even sweatier.

Chris wiped his forehead and rested his head in his hands to shield his eyes from the bright neon light in the room.

He felt the weight of it all overwhelm him slowly, like a tide coming in. He tried to suppress the tears, but it was futile, and his shoulders shook as he cried. Eventually even the tears ran dry, and he wiped his face with the back of his hand. He rested his chin on his fists and stared at the wall.

The door opened, and two people entered: a uniformed RCMP officer and a very smartly dressed woman. She had dark hair, a friendly smile, and emerald-green eyes. The freshness of her smell filled the room, and Chris tucked his arms closer to his sides in an attempt to mask his own pungent body odour.

The uniformed man was the first to speak. "I'm Officer Svenson. I need to remind you, as I said earlier, that you are here for questioning regarding the murder of Dr. Sheldon Peterson."

"Okay, but I didn't do it! It is so unfair. I was trying to help him. I don't know CPR, but I tried my best," Chris blurted out. "No good deed goes unpunished, they say. I'm the one who phoned 911—I'm the one that called you guys, didn't I? For heaven's sake, why would I call you if I was the one who did it?"

Chris was shaking with emotion, and the tears rolled down his cheeks again. He snorted back the mucus streaming from his nose.

Svenson pushed the box of tissues across the table with a sympathetic smile.

Chris looked up. "Thanks."

Officer Svenson nodded.

Chris blew his nose. "I was only trying to save him, but you want to pin it on me? Just like that? No other suspects? I don't wanna burn them, but in fairness, what about Ian and T? Have you even considered them?"

Svenson nodded and looked at his lady partner. "We are considering all suspects, Chris. That is why my colleague is here." He turned his attention to the woman. She acknowledged him with a quick nod.

"Thank you, Svenson. I'll take it from here."

Svenson nodded but didn't move. The woman smiled and turned to Chris. "My name is Catherine McBride. I want you to relax and allow us to help you. I'm here to see if we can figure out this whole confusing situation. Okay?"

Chris nodded.

"Is it okay if I call you Chris?"

"Yes, Chris is fine." He visibly relaxed in response to her soft, kind voice. He leaned back in the chair and wiped his face with tissue. He blew his nose again and threw the balled-up tissue toward the wastebasket in the corner. He smiled briefly when he made the shot.

Catherine smiled. "Score. That's a three-pointer," she chirped. "Okay, then. Mind if I talk to you about what happened?"

He nodded and lost his smile.

Svenson turned to her. "There are quite a few things brewing in the office. Are you okay if I step out?" he asked.

She looked at Chris and smiled. "Yes. As I said, I think we're okay. Aren't we, Chris?"

Chris nodded. "Of course."

"I'll be at the door," he said to her, but his eyes were fixed on Chris.

After Svenson had left the room, Catherine leaned over and pulled out a notepad from her bag. "Chris, why don't we hold off on the upsetting events and start with some background details first?"

"Okay."

"How old are you?"

"Thirty-one."

"How long have you lived on Vaseux Lake?"

"Since my parents died... So, since I was twelve."

"What do you do for a living?"

Chris smiled. "Nothing, really. I'm basically retired. My uncle died when I was twenty, and he left me everything: his house as well as his life insurance came to me. When I turned twenty-one, the money from my parents' trust also came to me."

"So, you don't *have* to work. How do you stay busy, then?"

"I do a bit of everything. I am a gardener, handyman, and maintenance man at Vaseux Lake. In the winter, I clear the snow. Stuff like that. People call me if there is a problem on the street, and I help out. I like it."

"Your house is the one at the very bottom of the street on the south end of the lake, isn't it?"

"Three-forty Sundial Drive, yes."

"And when did Dr. Sheldon Peterson and his wife, Angelique, move in next door?"

"Ten years ago."

"Did you get along?"

Chris looked down as he felt a warm tingle from the faint redness that crept up his neck. He shifted in his seat and took a sip of water from the cup on the table.

Catherine placed her pen on her notebook and sat back in the chair. She smiled faintly. "Oh, I see." She nodded. "And how long have you felt that way?"

"What way? What are you talking about?"

"It's very obvious, Chris."

Chris blushed. He dropped his red face into his hands to hide his embarrassment.

Catherine leaned forward. "How long have you loved Angelique?"

"I hate it when people assume stuff about me!" Chris snapped. He jumped up in anger. Officer Svenson stormed into the room.

"Sit down!" Svenson hollered as he stepped between Chris and Catherine. He had one hand out in front of him and the other on the Taser holstered at his hip.

Catherine got up and left the room while Svenson kept his eyes on Chris. Once Catherine was gone, he slowly backed toward the door.

Chris stood, unmoving but seething.

3

Ian was pacing the room like a caged lion. Every few minutes, he'd stop and holler a comment at the mirror, and at any officers who might be standing behind it.

"Come on! Get your shit together. I wanna go home!"

He banged on the door with his flat hand and pressed his face against the small observation window to see if anybody was coming down the hallway outside.

"Fuck." He dropped his volume and mumbled to himself, "Fucking cops and their power complexes. Guess that's why they choose the job in the first place, isn't it? To power-trip by controlling others. Bloody morons." He slumped back into the chair and shook his head. "Poor Chris. No good deed goes unpunished, as he would say. Help your neighbour, and you get the blame. Figures."

He looked at the clock on the wall of the interrogation room.

"What the fuck? Tick tock, assholes!" He drummed his fingers on the table and then walked up to the door to give it few more bangs. "Come on." He kicked the door. "Interrogate me if you want to, but fucking do it already." He placed his face against the porthole window to look down the hallway in an attempt to figure out what was going on.

Nothing happened.

He walked back to the chair and slumped down again. He had been in this repetitive routine for a while. Using the table as his drum set, he started to sing "I Want to Break Free," amusing himself with his own lyrics by substituting the *I* with *Ian*.

He drummed the table with flat hands in between verses, then upped the noise and sang at top volume. As he bellowed out about falling in love for the first time, the door opened.

Catherine and Officer Svenson entered, and Ian stopped singing midsentence, his drumming hands hovering over the table.

"Oh, you've fallen in love, have you?" Catherine said with a smirk.

Ian chuckled. "Nah. I avoid that love stuff. But of course, you *would* walk in right then."

"So I'm out of luck, then?" She winked at him as she put her folder on the table and pulled out her chair to sit down.

Ian leaned back in his chair, enjoying her opening salvo.

Catherine sat back and tucked a long, dark lock of hair behind her ear. She had a stunning smile. Ian was fixated on her mouth. He wore a quizzical expression on his brow as she made herself comfortable. Catherine squared her closed folder on the table and placed her blank notepad next to it.

"Hello, I'm Catherine. Is it okay if we have a chat? It's Ian, isn't it?"

"Indeed. Ian at your service. Do whatever you need to do. Let's get this fucking thing over and done with. I'm hungry, and it's been hours. I want to go home." Ian folded his arms as he leaned back in the chair. "I'm tired of this bullshit."

Catherine wrote Ian's name and the date and time at the top of the notepad. She threw a quick glance at Svenson.

"I have to inform you that you'll need to stay for a bit," Officer Svenson said to Ian.

"Why?" Ian snapped.

"We need to figure this out before anybody leaves. So stay calm. And stay seated."

Ian slowly got up and brought his face within inches of Svenson's. They matched for height. Svenson appeared larger due to the police vest, but both men were very muscular. Svenson had a slight belly. But he didn't flinch at the clear challenge. He kept Ian's stare. A few silent moments passed.

Ian spoke in a low, calm tone. "You don't fucking intimidate me, moustache man. If you were capable of achieving more in life, you wouldn't be a bloody cop. Don't take your inferiority complex out on me. Just another small dick in a uniform, I suppose. I could take you, you know, but you ain't worth the trouble."

Svenson clenched his jaw but remained motionless and silent.

They glared at each other for a few more moments before Ian leaned back. "Okay. I won't touch you or your precious, beautiful Catherine, but I am not fucking sitting down. This place is irritating me."

Svenson looked at Catherine. She shrugged. "Okay, Ian. I don't care whether you sit down or not. You can stand or pace if you want to, but can you promise to behave and remain respectful?"

Ian nodded and stared at Svenson. The officer's ears were still glowing red, and his right hand was still resting on the taser.

"Okay, boys. All done now? Territory all marked?"

Svenson and Ian nodded. Svenson leaned back against the doorframe, and Ian wandered a few yards to the mirror and back. He let out a long breath, put his hands on the back of his chair, and leaned in to make eye contact with Catherine. She calmly waited, seated in her chair.

"Okay. I'm all good. Ask your questions."

Catherine spoke in a kind, chirpy tone, and the volatile atmosphere evaporated immediately. "All right, then. Shall we?"

Ian nodded at her with a smile, but when he looked at Svenson, he gave him the middle-finger salute.

"That's enough, Ian," Catherine said in a firm, mothering tone.

Ian was clearly impressed. "I like that, Catherine! You've got backbone. Much more balls than numbnuts here."

"Stop, Ian," she said, unsmiling.

Ian lifted his hands and bowed his head. "My bad."

Catherine pulled her notepad closer. The room was quiet, and the chair creaked as Ian leaned heavily onto its backrest.

"Ian, how long have you known Chris?"

"Since we were about twelve."

Catherine paged through a folder. "Around the time that his parents died?"

Ian nodded. "Yes, that was the reason he moved to Vaseux Lake: to come live with his uncle. Tough time for

888

him. He cried all the time. That was when we started to hang out. He sort of leaned on me. I'm not a very touchy-feely guy, but we got along. I helped him with stuff like homework or sorting out the asshole bullies at school."

Catherine looked at her notes. "And you and T have been roommates with Chris for the last few years, right?"

Ian nodded.

"When did T join you two?

Ian leaned back for a moment. "About three years after Chris and I met: we were fifteen."

"How would you describe T in one word?"

"*Weirdo.*"

"Why do you say that?"

Ian shrugged. "Have you met the guy? How strange is the name, T, anyway?" he muttered. "I don't know how to describe him. Way different than me, for sure. Sometimes he irritates me: the smooth way he talks and his feminine mannerisms appear so put on and fake, but that's T for you. On the other hand, he can be very funny in a nerdy and clever way."

"But what do you find particularly 'weird' about him? It was the first word out of your mouth..."

Ian shifted his weight uncomfortably. "He gets paranoid as fuck. Like, weird."

"What would he be paranoid about?"

Ian rolled his eyes and lifted his palms to the ceiling as he shrugged. "Oh my God. Everything. Everybody. According to him, the world is out to get us some days."

"Can you give me specific details?"

"I don't want to dig up old stuff. He isn't like that all the time. I don't know. You'll understand how weird he is once you've spoken with him. T isn't a bad guy, he's just different. Maybe that would have been a better word to use." Ian wrung his hands and mumbled, "Why are we talking about T, anyway? You can talk to him yourself. Can we get this thing over with soon?"

"That's exactly what we're trying to do," Catherine said pointedly. "Why don't you tell me where you were yesterday?"

"I was home. Next thing I know, I'm in this cell, accused of killing my fucking asshole neighbour!"

Catherine was taken aback at his bluntness. She stared at Ian for a few moments. "Well. Clearly you didn't like Dr. Sheldon Peterson."

"Truth be told, I like very few people. But no, I didn't like Sheldon. He was an arrogant prick."

"Was his arrogance your main issue with him?"

Ian shrugged in a nonchalant way. "He snagged a young, beautiful woman—who was clearly out of his league—with his status and money. I think she was way too bloody beautiful for him. I mean, he was in his fifties, for fuck's sake."

"Do I sense a hint of jealousy, maybe?"

"Me? Of him? About Angelique? No way! Except she was clearly, truly meant for Chris. Angelique and Sheldon just seemed like an odd couple to me."

"It's difficult to judge those things from the outside, I suppose. However, I do get your point." She paused and then looked up from her notepad. "Did Chris and Angelique have an affair?"

Ian didn't flinch. A subtle smile pulled the corner of his mouth. "What is it with you, asking me questions meant for others? That one should go to Chris."

Catherine nodded. She leaned closer. "Okay then. Can I ask you something personal?"

"You can ask. I don't have to answer."

"You are correct. You say Angelique was meant for Chris, but I sense a lot of passion in your voice when you speak about her. Was there something between you and Angelique? Maybe I'm mistaken, but I sensed a little... something."

Ian shrugged. He remained silent.

"Okay. Let me be frank. You are a handsome guy with a strong personality. I'm pretty sure some women would appreciate that about you. And with Angelique living right next door, it makes me wonder... Did you two ever have sex?"

Ian gave her a quizzical stare, as if he were trying to determine if she was guessing or if she knew something.

"I have learned in life that people like you don't usually ask questions that you don't already have the answer for. And I don't want the truth to bite me in the ass later. So I'll be straight with you, Catherine, but you can't fucking tell Chris. Please."

Catherine nodded.

"I did have sex with her. Or, I should say, we fucked. It was an angry, wild fuck—not a love thing. She stormed into the house. Smashed a plate on the floor and yelled like a crazy woman. So emotional! Mad. Mad. Mad. She said her life was messed up. I was honestly clueless where the hell it all came from. She usually vents her shit with Chris, but he wasn't home. Her anger turned to lust. She grabbed me and... we were like animals."

Catherine tapped her teeth with the pen as she reviewed her notes. "When was this?"

Ian remained quiet.

"Come on, Ian. Was it recently?"

"Yes."

"How recently?"

Ian paced to the mirror and back. "Very," he mumbled.

"Ian. When?"

"Tuesday night."

"Three days ago."

"Yes," Ian said cautiously. "I know it sounds suspect, but I assure you it wasn't an affair or anything like that. She is Chris's as far as I'm concerned. It only happened because she was so angry... and maybe because she was very drunk."

"Can you recall more about what triggered her anger?"

"I really struggled to get a grip on it. She was babbling. She gets that way when she is intoxicated, but she said 'everybody lied to her' and now it was 'all fucked up'—whatever that meant."

"Lied about what?"

Ian shrugged and shook his head. "She didn't say. She was drunk. It was difficult to make sense of it. I merely allowed her to rant. It was all about Sheldon and his lies, and how he had 'fucked it all up.' No surprise there. I knew Sheldon was an asshole. There was no need to rub it in, so I let her deal with it. I kept quiet. It wasn't my problem. Not my monkeys, not my circus." Ian turned to face Catherine. "Why don't you ask her what the asshole Sheldon did?"

4

Twenty-four years earlier

"Mom, I don't want to go to school. I feel gross." Chris's voice was hoarse, and he offered up a few raspy coughs.

His mother put her hand to his forehead. "Let me see. You aren't hot. No fever. Go wash your face, and I'll make you some tea with honey and lemon. I think you'll be fine."

"Can I stay home?"

"No, Chris. You can't skip school because of a little cold or flu. There is a work ethic for everybody. Get ready for school."

"What does that mean—*ethic*?"

"Work ethic means you always go to school, even if you don't feel like it or you are a bit sick."

"Oh."

His mother sat down on his bed. "Chris, I am not trying to be hard on you, but we are not like other people who are lazy and skip out on stuff. I worked hard for my

PhD, and even though some might say I wasted that time to become a math teacher in a small town, that is not true. The knowledge I gained makes me see life differently. And I worked hard to have that education. Same with your dad. Have you ever seen him not go to work?"

"No."

"You see? The winery wouldn't be able to win all those awards if he didn't work so hard. The willingness to learn and work hard is the secret of success. Therein lies true happiness in this world. I don't want you to miss out on that."

"Okay."

"Get dressed. I'll make some tea."

Chris was quiet for a bit, and then he got dressed.

"Does Dad have a PhD too?"

"Yes."

"In winemaking?"

His mom laughed. "Sort of. Dad studied genetic engineering. How to make better grapes to make better wine."

Chris walked to school with a few tissues stuck in his pocket, but his snotty nose caused him to use them all within the first hour.

The class sat on the main carpet during story time. Suddenly Chris was blindsided by a big sneeze filled with green mucus. In an attempt to cover his embarrassment, Chris tried to wipe it off with his hands, but he only succeeded in smearing it all over his face. He stared at the pattern of mucus splattered over the back of Johnny Herbert, the boy who sat in front of him.

A stunned silence hung in the air as the snot dripped from his chin. Everybody stared at him. Chris feverishly dug in his pockets in search of a tissue but merely plucked out an empty tissue bag. His eyes begged for some assistance. However, the silent stares were followed by an avalanche of laughter. The teacher tried to shush them, but it was futile. Chris buried his head between his snot-covered fingers.

Angelique didn't laugh at all. Instead, she jumped up, quickly grabbed a bunch of tissues from her school bag, and sprinted back to hand them to Chris.

Chris grabbed the tissues and ran from the classroom to the farthest corner of the school grounds, crying. He was still wiping his face when Angelique sat down next to him.

She lightly rested her hand on his back as he sat, hunched over. "You okay?"

"No. But thank you for helping me."

"You're welcome. Are you going to be okay?"

"I dunno. That was the worst thing in my life," Chris mumbled.

"Oh." After a pause, she said, "But did you die?"

Chris looked at her, perplexed. "What?"

"Whenever I cry after getting hurt or something, my dad asks, 'But did you die?'"

Chris smiled. He snorted some snot. "I guess not."

"You'll be fine, then." She whacked his back playfully.

"Maybe."

"Sure you will. It's Johnny Herbert who's got a shirt full of snot! And he deserves it for always pushing people around." She laughed.

Chris laughed too. "Thanks, Angelique."

She shrugged as if it were nothing, but a new friendship was sealed.

Angelique lived a few blocks from school. After school, Chris's mom often gave extra classes for kids who struggled with math, so he'd walk home with Angelique. Spending time with her while waiting for his mother to finish extra classes was way more fun than hanging out alone on the swings.

Angelique lived in a small house on Bartlett Street. Her parents worked long hours: her dad worked for the railway, and her mom was cleaner. Chris rarely saw them, for they were either at work or sleeping between night shifts.

Chris and Angelique kept themselves busy by climbing trees, throwing rocks into the river, or building little boats from leaves and scraps and floating them down the river.

Near the time of Chris's seventh birthday, they were walking next to the river on a hot summer's day when Angelique had an idea: "Let's walk to that tow rope and see how far we can swing across the river!"

"I have always wanted to do that!" Chris replied.

Angelique stripped down to her underwear and ran to the tree. Chris dropped his pants, but then looked over at Angelique awkwardly. He blushed and decided to keep his shirt on. He pulled it down to confirm that it was covering his superhero underpants. Angelique climbed the tree and grabbed the rope. She pulled it back as far as she could. When the swing delivered her to its furthest point, she let go and flew through the air in an arc, splashing into the middle of the river. "Woo hoo!"

She surfaced, hollering, "That was awesome!" and swam to the side with a huge smile on her face.

Chris copied her every move. He grabbed the rope, stepped back, swung, and flew. He hit the water and disappeared.

Angelique waited for him to surface. Her smile waned, and then she panicked. "Chris? Chris? Why aren't you coming up?" She ran to the edge to see where he was.

Suddenly, he punched through the water's surface,

gasped for air, and went under again, thrashing. It was clear that he could not swim.

Panic-stricken, Angelique ran along the river shore as the current washed a bobbing Chris downstream. He would sink to the bottom, push off as hard as he could to launch himself to the surface, gasp for air, and go down again.

Angelique ran to an old tree with a low-hanging branch. When Chris bobbed by, she jumped in and grabbed him by the collar. Angelique was a strong swimmer. She pulled him to the surface and swam ashore, holding him by the collar with one arm.

They lay, gasping next to the river and shivering in the sunlight.

"Oh"—*breath*—"my"—*breath*—"God." *Breath.* "Why didn't"—*breath*—"you tell me"—*breath*—"you can't swim?" *Breath. Breath. Breath.*

When Chris eventually got his breath back, he answered.

"I thought it was something everybody could do. I didn't know you had to learn first!"

"What planet are you from?"

"I dunno. Thought we were born that way. It looked easy."

"Oh my God."

"What?"

"Chris, you are so weird... or special or something. How could you think that?"

"I don't know. Sometimes I know how to do things without remembering how I ever learned how to do them, but I guess swimming isn't one of those things."

She shook her head.

5

T watched the droplets run down one by one as the cold glass of water sweated a small puddle onto the table. He picked up the glass with his right hand and sipped it with his eyes closed, as if it were a fine Chardonnay. His left hand was snaking in the air as he conducted a melody he was humming softly. There was a smooth flow to his supple wrist movement. He reclined in the chair as if it were a La-Z-Boy, his legs crossed. An air of calm confidence surrounded him; he showed not even a hint of nervousness.

Catherine was trying to place the tune as she watched him through the one-way mirror of the observation room adjacent to the interrogation room. "Looks like T is waiting for us. What tune is he murmuring? Very famous... Might be Adagio in D, actually."

"Impressive," Svenson replied.

T glanced at himself in the mirror and rearranged his hair. His fingers continued to sculpt the air in flowing motions as the melody in his mind took him on a journey far away from the current time.

Catherine smiled and turned to Svenson. "Let's go see what the refined gentlemen has to say."

As the pair of investigators entered, T opened his eyes. His hands were still conducting the symphony orchestra in his head. He stopped abruptly and placed his hands on the table. His eyes were intense as he observed their entrance.

He made no secret of the fact that his focus was on Svenson.

"Yum. What do we have here?" He pointed at Svenson with an open, upturned palm. Mimicking a scanner with his hand, he slowly 'scanned' Svenson head to toe.

Catherine sat down, and Svenson remained standing by the door.

"Hi. I'm Catherine, and this is Officer Svenson. How would you liked to be addressed?"

He replied in a high, smooth tone, the words rounded and well enunciated. "Call me T for Ty, honey." He stretched out the 'honey.' He kept his gaze on Svenson.

"Okay." Catherine nodded.

"I was actually talking to the handsome Village People look-alike over there!" He grinned, amused by his own joke, and winked at Svenson. "But doll, that's fine," he said, turning his attention to Catherine. "We're all friends here. You're welcome to call me T as well, Catherine."

Catherine smiled. "Witty."

"I'd say. Served with a generous side order of sarcasm."

Svenson leaned in to speak to Catherine in a low tone. "You want me to stay?"

"Oh, please, do stay, Officer," T chirped in. Svenson blushed.

Catherine's gaze swayed with intrigue between the two men. She smiled.

Svenson nodded and stepped back, but he stayed in the room. T gave him a devious smile.

"Okay, T. Can we start?"

"Be my guest."

"How long have you known Chris?"

"I think roughly since we were fifteen."

"Why did you start hanging out together?"

T squinted at Catherine with suspicion. Then he gave her a broad, disarming smile. "I don't know. It's like any friendship, I suppose. We had common interests, and we complemented each other. He is shy; I am confident. He was pretty insecure when he was younger, and I could help him. And we weren't competitors, since we obviously bat for different teams." T winked at Svenson.

Svenson rolled his eyes toward the ceiling uncomfortably.

T laughed out loud. "Oh, for fuck's sake. I'm teasing, Officer Svenson. Don't sweat it. You're not my type—although the moustache and uniform do suit you."

Catherine smiled at Svenson.

"I find you very amusing, T." She smiled amiably, but she abruptly changed tack. "Let's continue. What are your recollections of yesterday—Thursday evening—when Dr. Sheldon Peterson got murdered?"

"I can't recall exactly. It was a very forgettable evening until the lights and sirens showed up."

She scribbled a note. "Did you see Sheldon yesterday?"

"Yes, in fact, in the morning. We left for a two-day bike tour the day before: Wednesday morning. We bikepacked the KVR, past Osoyoos. We slept in bivy bags under the stars on Wednesday night. I love the great outdoors. Seems unreal to think that was his last night alive. I guess you never know when your time is up. Life is strange that way."

"A bike tour? That's interesting." She scribbled another note.

T leaned back in his chair and slowly shook his head. "I have a strong suspicion that a clever detective like you, Catherine, would already have that information. Especially since I posted the entire ride on Strava—with pictures. And I know Sheldon posted a Relive video on Facebook that showed the whole ride. Thanks for being thorough and double-checking the facts, but let's cut the BS, honey."

Catherine ignored the tinge of sarcasm in his tone. "Oh, yes. I did see that."

"Of course you did." T smiled smugly.

"I assume that you and Sheldon were good friends, then?"

"You know what they say about people who assume—they 'make an ass of u and me.' But yes, we were neighbours, biking buddies, and friends, I'd like to think. He was an intelligent guy. An ER doc and all. We always had lots to chat about."

"What sorts of things?"

"Everything. I'm a bit nerdy. I read a lot, which is a rarity these days. We spoke about everything from interesting cases in medicine, to politics, to how stupid Trudeau is, to quantum physics and how the explanations for it kept slipping away from us both..."

"Anything more than that?"

T took a long pause. "How very *Brokeback Mountain* of you to ask."

"Yes, that is exactly what I'm asking."

T smiled. "Vegas rules apply to biking trips as well."

"What happens in Vegas stays in Vegas?"

"Yep."

"That was it? Biking buddies, nothing more?"

"You got it: biking buddies, friends, neighbours."

She sat back in the chair and tapped her pen on her teeth. The motion clearly irritated T because he abruptly looked the other way and glanced at himself in the mirror. When his eyes returned to Catherine, she was staring straight at him.

"Catherine, you are actually a very attractive woman. You have gorgeous emerald-green eyes."

"Thank you," she replied with a perplexed look. She shifted in her chair and leaned forward onto her elbows. A kind smile breezed onto her face and she asked softly, "T, have you ever truly loved anybody?"

"Yes."

"Was it Sheldon, maybe?"

T contemplated the question. "Maybe." He tilted his head slightly. "It depends on your definition of love."

"Let me ask you this, then: who do you care for most? If you could save one person in the world, who would it be?"

"Chris, of course."

"Of course?" She made eye contact with T. "Not Sheldon."

"I guess you don't get it." T smiled. "No. Not Sheldon."

She nodded. She paged through her notebook, checking a few facts, then mumbled to herself. "I guess we'll get back to that." She looked up and placed her folded hands on the notepad. "I am glad we finally met and it has been a long day, so I have a final question for now: did Chris murder Sheldon?"

T laughed. "Oh my goodness. Really? Have you met the guy? Do you know anything about Chris? I love the shit out of him, and you might think I'm saying this merely to protect him, but honestly, he couldn't hurt a fly." He leaned back in his chair and looked toward the big mirror as he swatted the air with the back of his hand as if to discard the ridiculousness of her statement. "Bloody hell. Not a chance. Not Chris."

Twenty-two years earlier

Angelique noticed Chris by the swings in the corner of the schoolyard. He was surrounded by a group of tough kids. The asshole-bully bunch had already eaten his lunch and taken all his emergency lunch money, and now they were having 'fun' with him.

"Are you a faggot, snotface?"

"Come on, you dick licker! Wuss! Get off the fucking ground!" The biggest kid leaned over Chris. "Are you gonna get screwed in the butt? Do you like it that way, you faggot?" He made pelvic thrusts in the air, and the group burst out laughing.

A tear ran down Chris's face. He didn't utter a sound.

"Whoa. Are those tears on your face?" the smallest one pointed out. He gave Chris a kick in the stomach. The rest of the group joined in immediately.

"Retards," Angelique mumbled.

She ran toward the group as they huddled over Chris.

Their backs turned toward Angelique, they were giving Chris their full attention. He was on his knees with his arms around his head to protect his face from their kicks.

Puberty had come early for Angelique. At nine, she was five feet—taller than all of the boys, who were still waiting for their testosterone to kick in.

As she approached, she scooped Chris's school bag from the ground. On arrival, she started to swing. She knocked the first two bullies over in one shot and kept going. Asking no questions, she exploded in a crazy rage: kicking, screaming, spitting, biting, stomping, and punching with the vengeance of a rabid dog. She literally foamed at the mouth as she swung the bag like a wrecking ball. She aimed at their nuts whenever they spread their legs. When she saw blood spray from a nose, it infused her with even more energy. "You stupid fuck-wits!" she hollered. "Leave him alone!"

They scampered away one by one.

Angelique kept kicking, screaming, and fighting until she was standing on her own. The bullies had fled. Chris was whimpering on all fours on the ground.

She helped him up. He had a black eye, and his lip bled. They sat there for a long while before Chris spoke.

"Why are they so mean to me?"

She shrugged. "'Cause they're scared coward assholes, and you're an easy target?"

"But why?"

"I dunno, Chris. That's just the way it is. Maybe some-body hurt them. Maybe they feel better if they give that hurt to someone else. Pass it on, sort of..." She put her hands up in the air. "But I honestly don't know."

"I try to be nice to everybody."

"I know. You are. But with people like that, it means

nothing. For them, it's all about whether they can kick your ass or you can kick theirs. They know nothing else."

Chris looked at Angelique as he contemplated her reply. He nodded. "I feel sorry for them, then."

Angelique shook her head as she smiled. "You are really too kind, Chris."

He shrugged. "Anyway, you kicked their asses. Thank you."

"I sure did! You wanna go have a swim in the river? We should wash that blood off your face before your mom freaks out."

"Yeah, we don't want that again. She made it all so much worse when she did that anti-bullying campaign thing the last time."

They didn't discuss the fight any further. They jumped into the river and drifted till they found their favourite spot. Chris was comfortable in the water as Angelique had taught him how to swim and float. Afterwards they dried out in the sun on the river shore. Then they skipped stones over the water. There was laughter and jubilation when Chris skipped his stone right over the creek and hit the big tree on the far side. They danced and hugged to celebrate.

7

Catherine and Svenson entered the office where Angelique was waiting. Angelique smiled in approval at the woman's intelligent and sophisticated look in her neat pencil skirt. Her eyes didn't linger on the bulky officer, who looked like an ogre to her in his tight-fitting uniform.

"Good evening, Angelique. I'm Catherine. Sorry for your loss."

"Thank you."

Catherine sat down across from Angelique. She had a thick notepad and folder in hand, but she placed them face down at the far end of the table and leaned in close on her elbows.

"How are you holding up?" Her tone was kind.

"I'm a mess." Angelique burst into tears, digging through her handbag for a tissue. She laughed suddenly, as if remembering something, and then she cried even louder.

Catherine tilted her head sideways at the emotional

turmoil on display. She pulled the tissue box closer and put it in front of Angelique.

"Thanks." Angelique blew her nose. She took a few deep breaths and appeared to settle down.

"Is this your office?" she asked Catherine, looking around.

"Why do you want to know?"

"Just wondering. I was staring at these walls for a while, waiting for you, and didn't think it was a woman's office. It is very neat, but there are no female touches—no offence intended, of course. Grey walls, a bookcase with RCMP textbooks, a computer, a lamp, and that's it. No family pictures. No art. No plants. Very clinical and neat but not homely at all. I notice stuff like that. Interior design was my 'job,' you know." She made air quotes with her hands. "I added the female touch to our house. Made it cozy. Made it a home rather than a bachelor pad. I did the same for Chris's place... and to be honest, I have a knack for it. My friends in town always asked me for my opinion, and I've even decorated some of the tasting rooms for the wineries. People drink more, stay longer, and buy more wine if they feel comfortable and at home. I thought this office needed my touch. It's a little plain and cold... Sorry. I truly didn't mean to offend."

Catherine smiled. "It's not my office, but I will pass on the message," she said with a sneak peek at Officer Svenson. She rearranged a few pages in front of her and then looked up at Angelique. "Emotions under control?"

Angelique nodded.

"What a terrible evening for you. I'm so sorry."

"Thanks."

"Mind if I ask you a few things? This investigation is a bit of a mess, and we are not clear about some details and how everything fell into place."

"Yes, I understand. Anything to solve this. What do you need to know?"

"First, let's take a step back in time. You met Sheldon when you were in nursing school, right?"

"Yes."

"You got married and then moved to Vaseux Lake?"

"Yes."

"Why Vaseux Lake?"

"I always wanted to come back."

"Because you grew up in this area?"

"Yes, in town. You know what they say: no roots, no flowers." Angelique smiled warmly as if to sell her answer, but Catherine frowned.

Catherine reached inside the folder, retrieved an evidence bag, and placed it in front of Angelique. The bag contained a pregnancy test. She quietly tapped on the little window of the test to bring Angelique's attention to the two dark black lines on it. The identifier on the bag read *Evidence Item #67. Location: garbage container at Sheldon & Angelique Peterson residence.* A picture was stapled to the evidence bag, showing a gloved officer holding the test in front of the garbage bin next to Angelique's garage.

Catherine spoke in calm but firm tone. There was no anger, only conviction. "Mind if we speak honestly, Angelique? You can spare me the BS."

8

Nineteen years earlier

"But what if he comes while you're away?" Chris hollered at his dad. It was a complete meltdown. But Chris's dad was better at handling it than his mom. Her analytical math brain could not deal with high emotion. Working with the taste and temperamental sensitivities of wine connoisseurs had taught Chris's dad how to deal with a sensitive son. He sat down on the bed next to Chris.

"You have become such a brave twelve-year-old. What made you worry about the Thin Man today?"

Chris looked at the window. "The wind is bad today, and one of his tentacles scraped the window. It screeched. Look! The Thin Man's arms..." Long, dark shadows danced on his curtains as the streetlight silhouetted the branches from the tall, leafless tree outside Chris's window.

His dad got up and opened the curtains.

"But look, Chris. It's only a tree. I'll turn on the outside light to take away those long shadows. Okay?"

Chris nodded. His dad walked out, and the outside light came on. The dark shadows disappeared.

His dad returned with the flashlight. "Remember this?"

Chris smiled. "My Jedi lightsaber flashlight."

His dad turned it on, and it blasted a beam of light onto the wall. "Yes. You remembered. Let's do a check like we used to, okay? Let the light chase the darkness and show us what is real."

Chris grinned.

"Cupboard?" His dad started the usual checklist.

Chris eagerly took the flashlight, pulled the doors open, and lit up the cupboard. "Check!" He smiled at the comfort this ritual brought.

"Behind the door?"

"Check."

"Under the bed?"

"Check."

"Down the hallway?"

Chris ran to the door and shone the light in both directions. "Left, check. Right, check."

"All clear?"

"All clear!" Chris hollered.

His dad spread his arms. "Come here, young man."

Chris ran into his dad's arms for the biggest hug in the safest place in his world. "Thank you, Dad," he whispered.

"You've got this, son. He won't get you. You are way too brave."

"And I have a strong light." Chris tapped the palm of his hand with the flashlight. "To chase away the darkness and show what is real..."

"Yes. That's my boy." His dad gave him another hug, smiling as the words he had repeated for years were quoted back to him. "Are you okay with us going to Vancouver?"

"Yes. I think so. Why are you going to Vancouver?"

"I told you. It's our anniversary, and I got tickets to the symphony."

Chris's shoulder slumped. "Augh."

His dad laughed. "I know you find the symphony boring now, but it's an acquired taste—it might grow on you. Anyway, this time you won't be joining us, and that's why we arranged for you to stay at Angelique's."

Chris nodded and smiled.

"You can call anytime and we'll come home, I promise."

"Promise?"

"Promise." His dad leaned in to touch Chris's nose with his own. As their noses touched, he repeated in a whisper, "*Nose* promise."

The next day, Chris's dad took the weekend bag his wife had packed and drove Chris to Angelique's house.

Angelique and her parents lived in a small, two-bedroom house with no extra bed for Chris in Angelique's room. Therefore Chris and Angelique made a big 'camp' bed in the living room with her mattress and the couch pillows. Around the bed they used sheets and furniture to build a huge fort. It was indoor camping, and Chris loved it. The sleepover was off to a good start.

However, on the Saturday night, Chris developed a high fever. In the past, fevers had made him hallucinate and brought the Thin Man to life. To add insult to injury, a huge winter storm was picking up. The blizzard winds turned all the trees outside Angelique's house into running Thin Men, with tentacle fingers that reached out and scratched at the windows to get in. As the storm intensified and the night grew dark, Chris became petrified. Angelique's parents were eventually able to settle him down by turning on all the outside lights, and finally he nodded off into a restless sleep, his flashlight clenched in his hand.

He woke up screaming in the middle of the night. "He touched me! A tentacle finger touched me!" He shone his flashlight around the living room, looking for the Thin Man that wasn't there. He was shivering and tremulous, burning up with fever. Outside, the storm was still raging.

Angelique ran to her parents' room.

Chris shone his light onto the mattress and noticed the big dark spot where he had wet the bed.

"No, no, no," he hollered, diving onto the wet spot to hide it from Angelique as she returned from the bedroom.

"What is going on, Chris?" Angelique's mom asked. She leaned over and touched him. "My goodness, Chris! You are burning up."

Chris didn't say a word. He sat on the mattress and shook with tremors.

"Did you have a bad dream? You certainly have a fever."

Chris nodded. "I wanna talk to my dad, please."

"Okay, but let's get you some fever medicine." Angelique's mom ran to the bathroom and returned a few moments later with some Tylenol.

"Can I call my dad, please?" Chris repeated.

"It is very late, Chris. Can't we call in the morning?"

"No! I wanna talk to him *now!*" Chris snapped.

Angelique gave her mother a pleading look. "Please?"

"Okay, Chris."

Angelique's mother shrugged and dialled the number on the house phone. She invited Chris to take the receiver by holding it out to him. But Chris remained firmly on the mattress on the floor. She frowned, but pulled the phone cord as far as it could go. She placed the phone on the mattress beside him.

"Hello?" Chris's dad answered.

"Hi, Dad."

"Everything okay, Chris?"

Chris started to cry. He looked at Angelique with pleading eyes. "Can I talk to my dad alone, please?"

After everyone had left the room, Chris sobbed over the phone. "The Thin Man touched me in my sleep, Dad. And the Thin Men have the house surrounded. They keep scratching the windows. They are coming to get me! They know you are not here, Dad! And Dad... Dad... I was so scared I peed the bed, and now the bed is wet, and I am at Angelique's house. I wanna go home. I want you to come get me. Please? *Please!*"

"Son, it's a long drive and it is the middle of the night."

"But you promised."

"I know Chris, but it is very stormy. The roads will be bad."

"But Dad, you *nose* promised!" Chris burst into tears.

There was long pause.

"Can I speak with Angelique's mom, please?"

"Angelique," Chris called out. "My dad wants to speak to your mom."

Angelique's mom returned and took the phone from Chris. "Hello. Are you sure? It's the Coquihalla," she said. "The weather is quite bad out here. Okay... Okay. Sure, I can do that. Drive safe!"

She hung up the phone. "Looks like your parents are coming home, Chris. Don't you worry. Just stay where you are." She walked out and returned with a towel that she wrapped around him as he sat there. "Your dad asked me whether we could give you a lukewarm bath. Angelique, would you go run the bath, please? I'll get some fresh sheets for the mattress. Fresh sheets make everybody feel better." She winked at Chris as Angelique left the room. "Your dad told me." Chris gave her a relieved smile and wrapped the towel tighter around himself. He got up after a few minutes and walked to the bathroom. The lukewarm bath and medicine broke the fever, and the fresh sheets *did* feel great. Nonetheless, the Thin Man remained outside the house all night. He constantly howled for Chris. Chris bravely walked to the window a few times. The outside lights left a perimeter of brightness, but the Thin Man lurked just beyond that. Chris would light him up with his flashlight beam, and the Thin Man would momentarily turn into a tree, but when the light moved away, he immediately reverted to a dark-faced, tentacled threat again, calling for Chris.

At first light, the Thin Men disappeared, leaving only trees buckled by the wind.

Chris finally fell asleep.

Later that morning, the phone in the living room rang. Angelique's mom rushed to answer it with a whisper. She hoped to give Chris extra time to sleep after his long night, but to no avail... She had to wake him anyway, for the police were coming over.

Chris rubbed his eyes, and when he finally got his bearings, he noticed the two uniformed officers sitting in the living with gloom in their eyes.

"Hey, Chris. I am so sorry to tell you this, but..." The officer swallowed. "Your mom and dad unfortunately passed away in a car accident last night."

Chris's eyes widened. "No, no, no!" He jumped up and looked out the window in disbelief, expecting to see their car in the driveway like his dad promised. "It was the Thin Man! He took 'em!"

Chris looked around the room in a panic, hoping it wasn't true. But everyone had tears in their eyes. Angelique's mom tried to comfort Chris with a hug. He hit her chest with the backs of his fists and tried to push her away. She held on to him until his voice suddenly turned from meek and whiny to angry and harsh. "Let me go! *Now!*"

She released him.

He wiped his cheeks with the back of his hand. "No one ever believes me. Now he took them..."

He put on his coat and shoes and walked out the door into the snow.

The officer looked at Angelique's parents in confusion. "What is he talking about? Who is 'he'?"

Angelique's mom sighed. "Chris has always been haunted by dreams of a scary guy he calls the Thin Man —like the bogeyman. He had a nightmare last night, and that's why his parents were coming back in the storm." She shook her head. "The ironies of life."

Chris stood under the big tree. His small figure, standing knee-deep in the snow, was dwarfed by the giant tree with its long, hanging branches nearly touching the ground in places. Chris stared up at the dark, monstrous form.

Angelique ran out and hugged Chris. "It's going to be okay."

"He is stronger than everybody."

"Oh, Chris." She hugged him as tight as she could.

"No one can fight him."

The only relative that the police and social worker could find for Chris was his mother's half-brother, George Williams. He lived in the last house on Sundial Drive on the south side of Vaseux Lake.

Although Chris liked his uncle's place right on the lake, he didn't really know George too well. Chris told the social worker that his dad and his uncle didn't really like each other and that he could remember a few arguments between them. All Chris knew about Uncle George was that he was a quiet man who lived alone. They visited him once in a while for a midsummer swim or Thanksgiving, but although he lived on the lake, he rarely went outside. He worked on his computer day and night.

Chris said his uncle smelled funny and had pale skin. He had a big beard and a long pinky nail. He mostly wore loose pj's, warm slippers, and the same red-checkered shirt. The social worker made multiple phone calls and left messages, but George never replied.

"He never answers the phone," Chris told her.

Chris was correct.

Eventually they drove to Uncle George's place with Chris in the back seat of the police vehicle. The officer knocked three times before Uncle George finally opened the door, and when the officer asked whether they could come inside, he gruffly said, "No."

A bit stunned, the officer remained courteous. Standing on his doorstep, the officer informed Uncle George about the accident and the death of his half-sister.

Chris overheard the conversation because the window of the vehicle was opened a sliver. He started crying again. The social worker next to him leaned over and hugged him. She closed the window.

Chris watched closely as the officer presumably

explained to Uncle George that he was Chris's only living relative. His message made Uncle George look at the police car anxiously and shake his head.

Eventually Chris saw his mouth move. "Whatever!" His uncle threw his hands in the air and walked back into the house. Surprisingly, however, he did not slam the door. In fact, he appeared to leave it purposely ajar. The officer cautiously pushed the front door open and called out for Uncle George. Then he shrugged and walked back to the car.

"Difficult to assess the guy. I don't know," he whispered to the social worker.

"Can we at least take a look around and see if it's appropriate for a child to live here?" she asked.

The officer shrugged. "Best we can do."

She grabbed the overnight bag Chris had brought to Angelique's. "Let's take a look, shall we?"

Her kindness made Chris cry. He left a wet spot of snot and tears on her shoulder.

As they entered the spacious log cabin, Chris took her hand.

The house was shiny clean inside. Uncle George called them to come upstairs. They walked through the big kitchen and living area, and peered through the large windows at a great view of the snow-covered lake.

They walked up the stairs.

"I've never been upstairs," Chris whispered. "It wasn't allowed when we used to come here."

The upstairs housed four bedrooms. Uncle George waited by the big room that looked out on the lake.

"Take this one. It has the best view."

The room was massive, with huge windows and even a small balcony.

The social worker appeared confused. "Are you sure? Isn't this your master bedroom?" she asked.

"It is, but I don't sleep here. I don't sleep much at all, but when I do, I usually sleep in my study downstairs. It's darker. This room is too bright."

"Wow. The view is amazing, isn't it?" She looked at Chris with real excitement.

Chris showed no emotion.

The social worker turned back to Uncle George. "This is great, Mr. Williams. Thank you for this. We realize it is very sudden..."

"These things usually are, aren't they?" he mumbled.

She put Chris's bag on the bed.

She leaned closer to Uncle George and behind a shielding hand, she whispered, "This is way better than any of the alternatives, so I personally thank you."

"Fine. It's blood, isn't it? Got to step up, like the officer said."

Uncle George turned to Chris and spoke a little louder. "Is this okay, Chris? We can arrange for someone to bring your other stuff over from the house. You'll need to tell me what you like to eat."

Chris shrugged.

Uncle George turned to the social worker with real distress on his face. "What does a twelve-year-old boy eat?"

She merely smiled. "You'll figure it out," she joked, as she patted his shoulder.

Flustered, Uncle George turned to Chris. "Whatever you want, tell me, and the grocery-delivery lady will bring it with my stuff on Tuesday. Okay?"

Chris nodded again.

Uncle George turned to the social worker. "I don't drive. How will he get to school?"

"I can send you the school district bus schedule. I'm sure there is a school bus that runs past here."

"Okay, then. Anything else I need to know?"

The social worker looked at Chris, who remained dead quiet.

"I guess that covers it." She shrugged.

Uncle George turned and walked down the stairs. They heard him close the door to his study next to the kitchen. When they reached the bottom of the stairs, they found the study door still closed. The social worker knocked lightly on the door.

"It's a no-go zone," Chris mumbled.

"What did you say, Chris?" She leaned toward him.

"Uncle George always told Mom and Dad that no one could go into his study. It was a 'no-go zone.'"

The social worker nodded. She spoke through the closed door.

"Well, I am going to leave now, Mr. Williams. Thank you for helping Chris. Please let us know if we can help in any way. I will leave my card on the counter."

"No problem," he replied from behind the door.

The social worker turned to Chris and ruffled his hair. "What do you think? Are you going to be okay here?"

Chris did a nod-shrug.

"Okay, then. This place looks very nice. I m sure you'll be okay." She pointed at the card on the counter as she walked out the door. "Call me anytime if you need anything."

Chris wanted to call her back, but he stood and watched the car door slam. His sigh deflated him until he was sitting down on the front step.

The social worker waved through the back window as police vehicle drove away. Chris watched the dust cloud roll out of Sundial Drive.

Eventually, he wandered to the water's edge and stared at his reflection in the lake. He became mesmerized as the ripples bounced against the edge and distorted his reflection. He didn't even notice the other boy till he spoke. The voice made him jump.

"Hey, did you see the turtles?" The boy looked about his own age, and he was standing nearby, pointing at the turtles perched on the driftwood a few feet into the lake. The kid was rough looking, and his eyes had a mean streak in them. Still, his voice was slightly friendlier.

"Hi, I'm Ian. Welcome to Vaseux Lake."

"I'm Chris."

Ian pointed at the turtle on the highest part of the stump.

"That big one over there is the leader. He's the lookout, my favourite. I call him Leonardo."

"Like the Ninja Turtles?"

"Of course." A sneaky smile formed in the corner of Ian's mouth.

Ian explained the who's-who of the turtles of Vaseux Lake, and Chris laughed at his stories about Leonardo, Donatello, Michelangelo, and Raphael.

"Where is Splinter? You know, their father who trained them?" Chris asked.

"They don't need Splinter anymore. These turtles are lean, mean, fighting machines!" And he made some wild karate chops with his hands. They both laughed as they sat next to the lake.

"This place could be pretty cool," Chris said.

"It's awesome. Let me show you around," Ian replied. "I'll show you the big tree over by the corner of the lake. I think we should build a tree house. Let's check it out."

They ran to the tree and started making plans for a

tree house, a zip line to zoom back to the shore, and maybe a tow rope to swing into the lake.

Chris beamed with excitement.

Over the next few months, their friendship grew, and Chris felt more and more at home.

Uncle George kept to himself most of the time, very rarely coming out of his study. Chris quickly learned that Uncle George wasn't angry; he was merely a hermit. He had a very set pattern. He stayed indoors all day, for he hated the sun. On the far side of the property, behind a clump of trees, he meticulously maintained a 'herb' garden. He dried the leaves from those herb plants in the small shed. Every day at dusk, he walked out onto the deck and smoked his dried leaves as he stared out over the lake. He mumbled to himself all the time, trying to solve some difficult problem or another. Chris could rarely make heads or tails of it. Sometimes Uncle George would get involved in loud arguments with himself. During those times, Chris would run off and play outside with Ian.

Ian didn't like Angelique too much and made himself scarce whenever she came over. It worked out fine for Chris, since he always had a friend to chat and play with, and there was no competition for his attention. Initially, Chris was scared that moving out of town would cause his friendship with Angelique to suffer, but Angelique's parents were great for bringing her over, and for organizing play dates or weekends by the lake. And Chris quickly learned the bus schedule to and from town.

After his parents' death, the Thin Man didn't bother Chris for a long time. Chris thought it was because of Ian. Ian was way stronger and tougher than Chris, and—as Ian himself used to boast—he 'took no shit from anybody.' At times, however, Chris thought Ian could be pretty mean. He had a raging temper, and occasionally Chris became the object of his friend's fury.

"We need to toughen you up, Chris," Ian would say. "Can't allow a girl to save you every time the bullies pounce!" Then he'd punch Chris hard on the shoulder or the legs. "Toughen up, you little wuss." He made Chris cry a few times.

One day they were sitting in the tree and planning their future tree house when, out of the blue, Ian grabbed the skin on Chris's leg. He gripped it so tightly that his nails dug into the flesh. Blood oozed. Ian yelled at Chris as he tightened his grip. "You'd better not cry, you sissy. I will punch you so hard you will regret every tear. Every single tear, I tell you. I am squeezing all the wuss out of you!" Chris responded by hollering in pain and squirming beneath the grip, but he refused to cry.

"Swallow the cement tablet, Chris!" Ian snarled. "Harden up. Okay?"

"Augh. Yes. Augh! Please. Please stop, Ian." Chris gurgled as his face contorted in pain.

"Are you going to cry?" Ian snarled as he squeezed harder.

"No," Chris said with conviction.

"Are you a wuss? Are you a crybaby?" Ian quivered as he leaned into his grip with all his strength.

"No, no. Please ssst..." Chris hissed out through a clenched jaw. A pain-generated sweat bead ran down his temple as he tremored in agony.

"Chris?" Uncle George hollered from the deck. He was outside smoking his herbs, when he heard the noise from the treehouse. "What is going on there?"

"Nothing!" Chris yelled back, fighting through the pain.

"Quiet down over there then."

"Okay!" Chris cried out.

"Well done," Ian whispered as he released his grip. "No tears." He tasted Chris's trickle of blood left under his finger nail by touching his index fingertip with his tongue. "You're getting stronger, Chris. Blood makes you stronger. Well done."

Chris hated Ian sometimes.

9

Catherine looked through the window in the door. Chris's outburst regarding Angelique had come and gone, and he was back to his normal, docile self, patiently waiting.

Catherine entered and sat down.

"Okay, Chris. You got all worked up before. I realize that the topic of you and Angelique is... How shall I put it? Sensitive."

Chris nodded.

"I'll let you in on a little secret." She paused.

Chris scrunched up his eyebrows.

She leaned in and whispered, "I don't mean to brag, but I'm really good at what I do. I specialize in assessing people's behaviour."

She paused to let that sink in. "Therefore, I know with one-hundred-percent certainty that there was something between you and her. She is a beautiful woman. I think there must be something exhilarating about having a secret affair with your neighbour's wife—a true friendship with benefits. The adrenaline and wild sex must be so addictive, I can only imag—"

Chris slammed his hand on the table and stood up. "Stop! It wasn't like that at all. Don't talk dirt like that about her!"

"Sit down," Svenson snapped. Chris responded immediately.

"Okay then, Chris. If it wasn't like that, then you'll need to tell me what it *was* like." Catherine's tone was suddenly smooth and comforting. She reached out and softly touched his arm. "Otherwise, I'll need to make my own assumptions. You understand?"

Chris nodded and stared into his lap for a while before he spoke. "We've known each other since we were six. We went through elementary school together, and she was my best friend—in fact, my only real friend. In high school, she matured faster than me. She was a bit of a tomboy. She liked doing boys' stuff with me, and she protected me from bullies.

"Then one day, she was chatting with me in the tree house. We were laughing about something silly and she fell over, right into my lap. And, boom! I had a... um... hard-on. After that, I couldn't look at her the same way anymore. She kept acting as if we were just friends, but from my perspective it was never the same. Suddenly her eyes, her hair, her smell—everything about her—mesmerized me. Not to even mention how it affected me when her breasts started to show and she turned into a real woman."

"When did it get more intimate between you? Do you recall the first kiss?"

Chris blushed. "I will never forget it. We sat in the tree house late afternoon one weekend she stayed over. We were joking about Uncle George and his weed-smoking routine. By then we'd figured out what the 'herbs' really were. We had snuck into his little weed-drying shed and stolen a few leaves. After smoking the joint, we were giggling about everything. We were laughing at the fact that he always wore the same shirt. I was in stitches when Angelique mentioned how she could always clearly see the silhouette of his dick in his pj pants. As our laughter died down, Angelique looked at me differently.

"She leaned in and touched my lower lip with hers. It was electric. Her lips hovered over mine, and then she took the smallest little nibble of my lip. I opened my lips, and she entered my mouth with her tongue..." Chris shifted in his chair and cleared his throat. "It was actually a very embarrassing experience."

Catherine frowned. "Embarrassing? It sounds very sweet to me."

"Not the kiss. My response. I had an immediate orgasm... in my pants."

"Oh."

"Actually, Angelique was really kind about it all. She giggled when I showed her the wet spot and said something like, 'Wow, what a compliment!' She was great about that.

"Anyway. Soon, our kissing turned to cuddles. Cuddles turn to fondles. Fondles turned to... uhm... anyway... serious stuff. Then, one Saturday in the fall, we didn't go to the tree house. We stayed in my bedroom and closed the door.

"We weren't worried about Uncle George, for he rarely left his study. I tried to put on a condom for the first time. I was shaky with excitement but clumsy as hell, and I could not figure out what the little tip thing was. She smiled and pushed me back on the bed.

"'Let me do it,' she said with a wink. She rolled it

down the shaft with ease and climbed on top of me. It was heaven. It was beautiful. I will never forget the warm glow of happiness that flushed to my brain as she slowly pushed me over the edge with her hips.

"Afterward, she lay next to me. We looked out onto the lake, naked, in stunned silence. 'So that's why everybody talks about it!' she whispered to me. I was fifteen.

"It was love. It was always love. Never anything else."

Catherine wrote some notes. She looked up. "That is so sweet." Then with sarcasm, she continued, "Really sweet, *but...*"

"But what?" Chris sat upright.

"As angelic as it sounds, I get the impression you're not telling me everything. I sense a *but* in your tone. What are you not telling me? What happened?"

"I don't know what you mean," Chris replied.

She squinted her eyes and circled something on her notepad. "Chris. There *is* something you are not telling me about the sex with Angelique. What happened?"

"*Nothing!*" Chris snapped.

Svenson's arm shot out and he pressed on Chris's chest to hold him back. Chris suddenly towered over Catherine. She didn't flinch.

10

I an was pacing. When he returned to the table, he placed his hands on the back of the chair and leaned forward to stretch his back.

"When is this going to end?" he snapped at Catherine.

"Well, hello, Ian," she said with friendly sarcasm. "I tell you, it is a tough puzzle to put all of this together."

"I bet. Especially with the help of dumbos like him." He pointed his chin at Svenson standing by the door.

"Hey. Easy, Ian. There are quite a few pieces of the puzzle missing. As I dig deeper, the Sundial Drive mystery keeps getting bigger. Quite a few secrets on that street."

"Maybe. Everybody has secrets."

"For sure, for sure. Maybe you can help me out. You are very close to Chris."

"So is Angelique."

"You might have a different perspective on what was really happening those first few years at the lake. I'd appreciate your take on things. What was the influence of their relationship on life in the neighbourhood?"

"What do you mean?"

"Well, I'm sure that when they started having sex, it must've changed the dynamic between you all. Chris is very defensive about it. He makes it sound like moonshine and roses, and my spidey senses tell me there is something he's not telling me. Can you tell me more about their dynamic after the sex started?"

"How am I supposed to know?"

"You and Chris have been close for years. I am sure you know him as well as anybody. Did something happen with him and Angelique? Sexually, I mean. Chris gets hypersensitive the moment we get to that subject."

"I'm not sure if this is what you're looking for, but I know Chris got really messed up after they were caught in the act."

"Oh boy—and he is such a shy guy. Caught by Uncle George, I presume?"

"Of course, and I predicted it. I told Chris he should do her in the tree house, but he preferred his bedroom. They kept doing it there and got a bit carried away. Or rather, *Angelique* got carried away, yelling and hollering, so Uncle George stormed in and caught them. Angelique loved sex, and she was wild from what I could deduce. In his defence, Uncle George might have thought she was getting hurt or something.

"Any which way, he stormed in and found Angelique bent over the bed with her hands held behind her back and Chris behind her. Uncle George hollered something and smacked Chris away from Angelique with the back of his hand. Chris crashed into the corner of the room and hit his head. After asking if Angelique was okay, he stormed out of the room, grabbed his belt, and returned.

He threw Chris on the bed, pushed his face into the linen, and laid into him with the belt.

"He went overboard on Chris's ass, beating the shit out of him. Fuck, he must've thought Chris was raping Angelique or something. Finally, Angelique was the one who jumped onto Uncle George's back and choked him till he stopped.

"After that, Uncle George rarely allowed Angelique to visit, and he watched them with a hawk's eye whenever she did come over."

"Appears a bit excessive, doesn't it?"

"Uncle George was very worked up, for sure. He said it was 'indecent' and that it wouldn't happen under '*his*' roof."

"What are your thoughts on that?"

"It was ridiculous. Teenagers have sex," Ian said in a nonchalant way. "I couldn't really figure what was so horrible about that. He didn't need to beat Chris up so badly. You should've seen it. Chris was black and blue all over his back and butt. He walked like an eighty-year-old for three days. It was crazy."

"Did that incident stop the sex?"

"Of course not," Ian said, rolling his eyes, "but at least they became much more cautious about it, like having an affair. Nonetheless, Angelique did visit less. I enjoyed the extra time with Chris, but I think he missed her a lot."

Catherine paged through her notebook. "Was it around *that* time that T joined the friendship?"

"Yep. With the girl gone, the faggot joined." Ian smirked.

"Please! Be nice," Catherine said sternly.

"Hey, I like the guy. I'm just being honest. No secrets here."

11

The positive pregnancy test lay between them on the table as Angelique stared at Catherine in silence. Catherine met her stare and then shook her head with a foxy smile. She scribbled a little on her notepad and placed it back on the table. Face down.

"Okay, Angelique. We both know the significance of this test, but let's first step back to you and Chris. You were best friends in elementary school, right?"

Angelique nodded and tucked her hair behind her ear.

"And then high school came, Chris's parents died, and he moved to Vaseux Lake to live with his uncle."

Angelique nodded again.

"Things between you and him changed then, didn't they? He told me about your relationship, but I'd like to know how you experienced it."

Angelique nodded and opened her mouth to talk, but before she uttered a sound, Catherine lifted her hand to stop her.

"Before you start..." She looked over at Svenson. "Officer Svenson, do you mind stepping out for a moment? I think this might get very personal. Maybe give us ladies a few minutes?"

He nodded and left the office.

Angelique took a moment and closed her eyes as if she were travelling back to her pleasant youth. "God. How do I describe it? We were young. It was mostly innocent teenage love." She paused.

"What exactly do you mean by 'mostly'? It wasn't all sweet and innocent? Was it different sometimes?"

"Once or twice. The first time was very... um..."

"Awkward?"

"Rough."

"Oh." Catherine nodded. "Please continue."

Angelique looked at her hands.

"I think the details are important here. It's just me and you," Catherine urged.

Angelique sat back to relive that moment, and Catherine watched her closely. A warm, red blush rose up Angelique's neck.

"We were smoking some weed from Uncle George's grow op. It was a usual weekend visit. I guess we were fifteen. Just chilling in the tree and swinging from the tow rope into the lake. We were wet, and as we climbed back into the tree house I recall his uncle hollering from the deck, 'Hey, what are you two up to?' I giggled from the weed, but Chris hollered back, 'Nothing!' and pushed my butt hard to shoot me into the tree house. He quickly scurried in too and closed the hatch. I lay on my back, giggling, and he stood up and looked down at me in a very strange way. He said nothing. He just dropped his pants, displaying his hard penis. He leaned over, put his hands on my bikini bottoms, and took them off in one swoop.

"'What is this?' I asked—rhetorically. I sort of giggled. I played coy by bringing my knees together. He put his hands on my knees and pushed them apart forcefully. He spit on his hand and rubbed me with it. Then he lined himself up and came at me. Hard. A searing pain ran up my back as he tore me inside. My eyes widened, and I screamed out, but it was muted by his hand over my mouth.

"He took control of me. He withdrew his blood-covered shaft, looked me in the eye, and then forcefully shoved it right back in. Eventually, he took his hand off my mouth and ordered me to remain silent by touching his lips with his index finger. I clenched my jaw, refusing to yell out from the pain. We maintained silent eye contact as his hips picked up a rhythm.

"It was a very strange experience. I hated and loved it at the same time. I shied from the pain, but adored his new-found horny sexual authority and strength. Chris had suddenly become a man. My friends said their first time was clumsy or laughably non-passionate. Mine was nothing like that... It was wild."

Angelique stared into space.

"Steamy, but on the edge of rape?" Catherine commented.

Angelique snapped awake from her daydream. "Oh my God. Sorry! Yes. It was very rough, wild... like animals. I exploded with a huge orgasm. It was so unexpected, I thought I'd peed myself. Our first time was unlike anything I would have expected." Angelique laughed awkwardly. "Total embarrassment, total satisfaction, and complete happiness, all rolled into one wonderfully strange moment in time."

Catherine scribbled vigorously.

Angelique touched her warm cheek and giggled. "I'm flushed. Maybe a bit too much information for public consumption."

"No, I appreciate the candour. It helps a lot. All in all, it sounds like it was pretty violent."

"Uhm, 'violent' isn't the right word." Angelique tilted her head backward. "*Passionate* would be a more appropriate word, I think."

Catherine paged through her notes, looking for something. "You know what I find interesting? Chris recalled that first time completely differently. In fact, he even claimed that it happened in his bedroom."

"Of course he did." Angelique smiled knowingly.

"Care to explain?"

"Chris never talked about it afterward. Maybe he was too embarrassed. You must understand Chris. He was going through a tough time. We were in love, but to him, a wild round of passionate sex was somehow dirty or bad. He probably told you about the second time and omitted the wild first time. The second time, we did it in his bedroom. I brought the condoms from town because I was very freaked out that I'd get pregnant after the tree house episode."

Catherine nodded. "To recap, then: you think he truly wanted the first time to be innocent, beautiful, and intimate—and you think he told me that white lie to make it so in his memory?"

"Chris is like that." Angelique nodded. "He doesn't mean to lie, but sometimes when something is awkward or painful, he simply blocks it out and moves on as if it never happened. In this case, I think he didn't want you to degrade our relationship to something bad or dirty."

"Hmm." Catherine frowned.

"Can I ask that you please give Chris some leeway here? He was very conflicted during that time. His parents were dead, and he'd been left with his weird-as-fuck uncle. He had no role model to help him find himself. We used to talk about sexuality all the time, and he even had moments when he thought maybe he was gay. I asked him why, and he said, 'No reason,' but he was concerned. Chris was uncertain about everything—like most teenagers, including myself. He was idealistic about love, and the whole conflicted teenage phase was exceptionally hard for him. He is no liar. I am sure in the ideal world in his mind, it was just the way he described it to you." Angelique took a sip of water. "But memory can be a fickle thing."

"It sure can be." Catherine nodded slowly. "Speaking of finding sexual direction in life... Did you experiment with that?"

"What do you mean?"

A brief smile from Catherine. "You're playing innocent here. Did you ever hook up with a girl, or were you convinced you were heterosexual all along?"

"Shit, you are a straight shooter!"

"No point in beating around the bush," Catherine replied with a guileful smile.

They both giggled.

"I kissed Sara Dressler in the girl's bathroom after hockey. It tasted cool, but I knew it wasn't for me."

"And to your knowledge, did Chris ever experiment in that way?"

"I doubt it. Chris is an analytical thinker, and he certainly would not have had the courage to grab another boy in the locker room. To be honest, even if he had, and even if that boy were actually gay, Chris would probably still have been beaten to a pulp in Oliver. It was the small-town conservatism we grew up with. So I'd say no. The bullies already had his number. I doubt he'd have risked it."

"How long did he stay conflicted?"

"Hmm. You'd have to ask him, but when we started having sex, he stopped talking about it."

The room fell silent except for Catherine's scribbling. "Okay. Let's talk about you and Sheldon. You met him when you were in nursing school, right?"

"Yes." Angelique shifted uncomfortably in her chair, and it creaked.

"You were together for about ten years, right? How was your relationship recently?"

Angelique shrugged. "Domesticated. We both did our own thing."

"And the intimacy? Did you still have a sexual relationship with Sheldon?"

"Sex between me and Sheldon?" Angelique sighed softly. "It was basically non-existent."

They both looked at the pregnancy test still lying on the table.

"Yep. I know. Life throws some strange curveballs sometimes."

There was a long silence.

Catherine was fidgety as she flipped through her notebook pages. "Then let's leave that topic for the moment. Can I ask you something completely different?"

"Sure."

"There was an incident when Uncle George gave Chris the beating of a lifetime after he caught you guys having sex. I understand Chris was all black and blue. Can you shed some more light on that?"

"Augh. I wish I could just forget about that. Yes, it was

quite an incident. Uncle George was livid. I had to pull him off Chris."

"Why do you think he reacted that way? Did he not expect you guys to have sex?"

Angelique shrugged. "I really don't know. Maybe." She put her hands up and shook her head. "But everybody knew Uncle George was totally, fucked-up crazy."

"Could you be more specific? Why do you say that?"

Angelique tilted her head with a quizzical expression. "Well, that's what everybody said. I am no shrink, so I can't really tell you much about him except that he was a recluse who *literally* creeped around the house. He freaked me out, even before he basically banned me from visiting Chris. The house is big, as you know: four big bedrooms on the top floor with beautiful views. But he stayed in the basement study with his computers and cot bed. Weird. He never came outside. He barely ever spoke, and when he did, it was usually just to mumble to himself."

"Why 'crazy,' though?" Catherine made air quotes with her fingers. "Did he appear mentally ill, as in confused, psychotic, or drugged out at any time?"

"No, not really. He smoked his regular joint in the evening, but I saw no other drugs. I would say he was strange and eccentric. On the one hand he obsessed about the house being clean, but in contrast, his body odour clearly suggested that he didn't wash himself often. He mumbled like a super nerd, a crazy professor. It was all academic, like Stephen Hawking. I do think he was into quantum physics, theoretical physics, high math— something like that—and his brain functioned on a different plane. He said that our 'sex noises' broke his concentration, and that was why he gave Chris that beating."

Catherine nodded. "And then his death was strange as well. A peculiar accident, right?"

"Yes. I don't know all the details, as I was away for my second year of nursing school when he died. It was a freak accident. He was struck by lightning." She paused to recall. "Chris told me the story. Their little dog, Mitch, ran outside during a thunderstorm and got his leash snagged around the zip-line post. Lightning had struck a nearby tree, which brought the high-power cable down onto the zip-line cable. Uncle George ran out to get the dog, but when he touched the charged zip-line post, he got electrocuted. I think there was a big BC Hydro investigation."

"It appears even in death, he was odd," Catherine commented.

"An 'act of God' was the investigation's conclusion, I heard... and I'd tend to agree. George was not nice. Maybe that was why God acted."

Catherine scribbled some notes. Angelique stared out the window as the sun stared to set.

"And the dog?" Catherine asked.

"Poor thing... Little Mitch. The cutest little Peke-a-tzu!"

"What breed is that?"

"It was a Pekingese–shih tzu Heinz 57 that Chris adopted a few years prior. He found the little one dehydrated and whimpering on the side of the road. Uncle George tried to find the owner by placing ads in the paper, but no one replied. People travelling through must have simply abandoned it. It was in horrible shape: sickly and malnourished, with patches of hair missing from fungus and infection. Uncle George and Chris nursed the little bugger back to life. It was close to the end of Grade 11, and I can clearly recall the scrawny thing. It looked like a dying, wet rat when Chris saved it. I think its growth was stunted due to malnutrition, for it was miniature-sized, even for the breed.

"Strangely, this dog became Uncle George's little shadow. He even slept with Uncle George in his study dungeon. If Uncle George ever loved anything in this world, it was that dog. Mitch whimpered occasionally but never barked. When he patrolled the house, he would always skirt the walls and furniture—he never crossed the room through the centre of the open space. The poor dog was deathly scared of storms and thunder. I understand why an intelligent person like Uncle George, who barely ever went outside in normal life, would rush out during a lightning storm to save poor Mitch. They say he had Mitch tucked to his chest in one hand when he touched the charged zip-line post with the other. They both died on the spot. Tragic. Well, tragic for Mitch. Nobody really missed Uncle George. But Chris cried for days over Mitch. He called me in Calgary, in tears. He was hollering that Mitch had died, and it actually took me quite a few minutes to figure out that Uncle George had died as well!"

"You said that was your second year of nursing school?"

"Yes."

"So you and Chris were both twenty?"

"Yes."

Catherine stopped and looked at her folder. She paged through some paper and then nodded. "Okay. The suicide attempt makes sense now," she mumbled to herself.

"What? Who?" Angelique abruptly leaned forward.

"You know. Chris's suicide attempt."

"What are you talking about?"

Catherine looked stunned. "Sorry. I was sure you'd know about that."

Angelique shook her head vigorously and burst into tears.

"I'm really sorry. Yes, Chris tried to commit suicide a few weeks after Uncle George's death. He tried to hang himself. He was admitted to the mental health unit for a while." Catherine looked at her notes. "Here's the hospital admission note. He was committed under the Mental Health Act and stayed in hospital for evaluation for two weeks. This event appeared odd, for we are all well aware Chris wasn't really close with Uncle George. I didn't really make sense to me. I thought maybe it was the loss of his only family member that triggered it... But that didn't sit right with me. Now I realize the attempt was triggered by the death of Mitch, not Uncle George. Chris must've missed the little dog companion! And with you away, he perhaps felt even more isolated."

Angelique put her head in her hands. Her blonde hair hung like a curtain between her and Catherine. "Fuck," she muttered. "That explains the wedding issue."

"What wedding issue?"

Angelique reached for a tissue and blew her nose.

"Around the time that Uncle George had passed, Sheldon proposed to me. I called Chris repeatedly. I really wanted to talk to him because I needed his opinion about me marrying Sheldon. I left him a ton of messages on the answering machine. Now I know why he never replied or came to my wedding. Obviously he couldn't: he was admitted to the mental health hospital. But I never knew. I can't believe he never told me." Angelique shook her head in disbelief. "Anyway, Sheldon and I eloped for the wedding. We each invited a few close friends and flew to Cancun on a whim. It was romantic and impulsive.

Chris never gave me a reason for not attending. He simply said afterward, 'I couldn't make it—sorry.' I was mad at him for years. I guess we never know everything about somebody else."

Catherine nodded. "I see that every day."

12

Upon entry, Catherine sat down but remained silent.

"Pardon me. Could you give me a moment? I need to recap some details," she said. She played with her necklace and attentively paged her notes.

T watched intently as she twirled the large emerald on the gold chain. After a while he started to soft hum a symphony tune. He glanced at himself in the mirror and re-arranged his hair.

Eventually, she looked up and placed the gold chain back on her chest. "Hello T, I must admit, you are a difficult guy to connect with. But let's give it a shot. Are you ready for a few more questions?"

T spoke with his distinctive smoothness. "I'm all yours, Catherine. No deliciously hunky officer this time?" He leaned back in the chair, crossed one leg over the other, and rested his hands on his thigh. His foot had a slow bounce to it like a metronome.

"I don't want any distractions," Catherine replied.

"For him or for me?" He chuckled at his own joke. He leaned forward and folded his wrists over his knee.

"Funny," she said with wry smile. "Now allow me to cut to the chase. I am trying to figure out more about Uncle George, and I figured you might be the one to help."

"Honey, you are right. I *do* know a thing or two, but why would you think I'd know more than the others?" His pitch was noticeably high, causing the 's' to slice the air.

Catherine looked up after checking her notes once again. "Let me tell you how I have perceived you thus far, T. You strike me as a clever guy. I sense that you are cautious when you meet people. Your eyes analyzed my every move and weighed every word I said from the get-go. I think it's fair to say that you don't trust people easily. You might even be a bit paranoid. How am I doing thus far?"

"I *am* impressed," T replied with smirk.

"I respect those characteristics, for I tend to be cautious and analytical of others as well."

T nodded.

"Since we share those meticulous qualities, I'd like to know your impression of Uncle George."

"'Eccentric intellectual' was my first thought. Clever, nerdy guy. I sat down with him, and he explained some of his theories to me, but I could not follow him very far. It was way beyond my knowledge base. Some days I thought he had a Nobel Prize hidden in that skull of his, but on other days, nobody was home."

"Care to explain?"

"It's difficult. You know when you're not sure if someone is saying the cleverest thing ever or talking complete horseshit? He operated at that level. The level where geniuses hover and converse while the rest of us think they are nuts."

"What was your final verdict? Do you think he was mostly genius or mostly crazy?"

"I think he was a freaky genius."

"Pity to have lost such a brain, then, and to such a tragic accident. Maybe the cure for cancer or intergalactic travel was lost..."

"Tragic? I would not call it that. Losing poor Mitch was tragic, but not George. Bottom line: Uncle George was a creep."

"Pardon me?"

"He might have been a genius, but he was mostly a creep. He won't be missed."

"A creep?" She squinted. After a long pause, she leaned in and whispered, "What kind of a creep are you talking about? What was up with Uncle George?"

T was quiet for a while. "Chris cannot know that I told you this. But whatever that suspicious mind of yours is conjuring up... is the truth. Did Chris tell you about his fear of the Thin Man?"

"No."

"Well, Chris had this fear of the bogeyman. He called him the Thin Man. Years later, when the whole Slender Man meme was circulating, Chris said that Slender Man was the Thin Man. Chris was also convinced that the Thin Man somehow caused his parents' death. It was a massive fear of his, but deep down he hoped that the Thin Man was only a manifestation of his nightmares and anxieties.

"Then he moved in with Uncle George. And one night he woke up with that fucker right behind him in bed, touching him. Chris realized that Uncle George was the *actual* Thin Man of his childhood nightmares.

Suddenly the puzzle made sense: Uncle George used to babysit Chris when Chris's parents went away for weekends. After every weekend away, Chris would be a mental disaster: peeing his bed, having nightmares, clinging to his big flashlight—all in fear of the Thin Man. I think his parents must have suspected something because they scaled down the visits with Uncle George at some point. They arranged for him to stay instead at Angelique's parents on their weekends away. I think it's fucked up that Chris was essentially forced to move in with his pedophile uncle."

"Oh my God, that's horrible." Catherine shook her head and made a note. "However, it could have been an honest mistake by the social worker. Especially if none of this was officially reported or documented. In the end the fact was that Uncle George was Chris's only living family member. It would only be logical for Chris to be placed there. But why didn't Chris speak up? Or why didn't *you* speak up on his behalf?"

T made a grand theatrical bow to confirm Catherine's words. "My thoughts exactly! I told him to speak up, but he was too ashamed and embarrassed. When I came on the scene, it had been going on for years, and Chris said he was sort of used to it. He was an intelligent boy. He realized that with no other relatives, he'd go to a foster home if he spoke up, so he chose the devil that he knew. It is unacceptably fucked up... But it is the way it is."

"That is so sad. It's maddening."

"That's why Chris was conflicted about his sexuality. Secretly, he told me, not everything that he experienced with Uncle George was bad. He was freaked out by the fact that he liked some of it. Maybe it was the closeness and comfort at times. Of course, after Angelique had sex with him, he started to resist Uncle George more..."

Catherine scribbled a note as she nodded. "That explains the beating of Chris and banning of Angelique after he caught them."

"Of course. In that instant, Uncle George suddenly understood why Chris had grown cold toward him."

"Did Uncle George leave him alone after that?"

"Come on, Catherine. What do you think?"

Catherine dropped her head. "Of course not."

"Yes. Of course not. It became less frequent, but less consensual as well. Uncle George went pretty rough on Chris sometimes."

"And nobody spoke up?"

"It was Chris's call, and he was in turmoil. After a bad round, he'd be on the verge of calling the police, but he didn't want to be ripped from the house or go into foster care."

"Did Angelique know about the abuse?"

"No way."

"And Ian?"

"Doubt it."

"Why do you think so?"

"Well, Ian gets *so* freaking angry, *so* freaking quickly," T said as he rolled his eyes to the ceiling. "With that temper, he would've beaten Uncle George to death..." T smiled sneakily as he covered his lips with a flat hand. "Oops. Bad choice of words in context, I guess."

"Maybe. But seriously, do you think he killed Sheldon?"

"Who? Ian?"

"Yes," Catherine answered briskly.

T watched his foot bounce. "I don't know. It is always a possibility. That's why he's a suspect like me and Chris, isn't he? The scene was violent enough for his tempera-ment, but the question is *why*. Why on earth would any of us want to kill our neighbour? Honestly, honey—we live two hundred yards from a major highway. Have you even truly considered any other suspects?"

"We are looking at all options. I was only asking about Ian."

"Fair enough. You had to ask. And I know Chris had blood on his hands, but he was trying to save the guy, for heaven's sake." T's tone turned sharp, clinical, as he leaned in close to Catherine. "Even though you appear sharp, your actions in this case leave a bit to be desired." He shook his head in disbelief and drummed his fingers on the table.

Catherine crossed her arms and sat back in her chair. "Okay then, Mr. Clever. If you were us, where would you look for Sheldon's murderer? What would you do differently? Did he have any secret enemies that no one is telling us about?"

"Well, it was a passionate kill, and passion suggests love or jealousy. A knife right between the eyes, right down to the handle. I'd say that's very passionate—nearly intimate—wouldn't you?" T said.

"Yes." Catherine nodded. "That is why we look at people who knew him well. Who lived close by…"

"Well, I'd be looking for a disgruntled ex-lover. Have you even considered screening the guys on Sheldon's Grindr account?"

Catherine's head jerked up. Her jaw was clenched. "Grindr?"

T smiled in satisfaction. He folded his arms. "Yes, honey. Very much a Grindr, I'd say."

13

Catherine walked into the office and slumped into the chair. She gave Svenson a stern look.

"Bloody hell, Svenson. I hate getting blind-sided!" She rubbed her forehead vigorously. "Sheldon on Grindr, a gay pickup site... I didn't really consider that angle. That changes a lot." She massaged her temple for a moment. "So Sheldon was a senior emergency physician working in Calgary. He met a young nurse and eloped with her, but all along he had an interest in the gay scene?"

"Maybe the gay angle was more about novelty and excitement? Bisexual."

Catherine shrugged. "You know what they say: bi now, gay later. We need to know more details about the state of his relationship with Angelique. Also, we need to dig through his social media accounts and check for Grindr hookups, et cetera. Vaseux Lake is en route south to Osoyoos and the USA. Lots of men would travel through looking for a fun night. Focus especially on the regular or repeat hookups. Somebody who might have gotten jealous or wanted more."

"I'll get an officer on that."

"What has forensics delivered so far? Anything new?"

"Lots of little details. There was no sign of breaking and entering, but on the flip side, all the doors were either open or unlocked. It is not a high-crime area. Full autopsy report is not out yet, but preliminary is that the stab to the face caused him to bleed out."

"Hmm. There was a lot of blood. I wonder how much blood you actually need to lose to die. Sorry. Random thought. Anything else?"

"Actually, a couple of things. There is a partial fingerprint on the knife handle. We are looking for a match. And the victim was stabbed in the face, but he also had a cut to the palm of his hand..."

"Well, that's not unexpected. In self-defence, most victims would get lacerations to the hand."

"I know, but the weird part is that he had tissue paper wrapped inside his hand, over the cut."

"Are you saying that he was trying to stop the bleeding in his hand—while he had a knife stuck in his face? That makes no sense."

"Exactly. A period of time must've elapsed between the hand injury and facial one. Enough time to grab some tissue paper, anyway. We are looking at separate injury timelines there. Let's see what the blood-spatter analyses show."

Catherine made a note in her notepad. "Okay, I will have another chat with Angelique about her and Sheldon."

"Sure." Svenson nodded.

"Oh, and maybe you can get somebody to review that BC Hydro investigation report or talk to someone about the Uncle George accident? I think we need to recheck that. This 'act of God' thing bugs me."

"Will do." Svenson added that to the list in his pocket notebook. "What are your current thoughts on Sheldon's death: which one, do you think, did it?"

Catherine tapped her teeth with her pen and tilted her head back. "Here is my current train of thought." She started playing with her necklace, watching the emerald twirl at the end of the gold chain. "I think the case against Chris is a slam-dunk, but only circumstantial. If you wanted to convince a jury, I think you'd have a fair chance of a guilty verdict. However, I don't think he has it in him. I don't feel it. Look at his temperament. He is timid, broken, weak, shy. He does not strike me as a guy to bury a knife in someone's face."

"What about Ian?"

"With his aggression, he makes me wonder, but I think we need to find a motive. He is very principled."

"T?"

"Not really his style, is it? I wouldn't put it past him, but it appears way too messy for someone so calculated in everything he does. Look at the way he talks, moves, and interacts... The murder scene does not fit his character *at all*."

"Are we missing something? And more importantly: what about Angelique?"

"Yes. I need to talk to her again. There's too much I don't know. She is hiding some truths for sure. Would you send her in on your way out? She's in the waiting room. And look into those Grindr dates. Casting the net wider is the way to go here."

"On it."

14

Catherine was slowly moving side to side by pivoting the office chair. Twirling her necklace, she looked at the office and smiled at Angelique's observation from earlier. There was, in fact, nothing distinctive about Svenson's office. Nothing personal; all work. RCMP books on the bookcase. No family photos. Not even a social screensaver on his computer. The standard time-and-date icon floated across the black screen. His desk was neat. All the cases he was working on were locked away in the file cabinet to her left. Catherine's curiosity was tweaked. She opened the drawers of the desk and looked for any signs of life outside the RCMP office. Except for a letter opener with an elk at the end, indicating that Svenson or someone he knew was a hunter, she found nothing. Catherine frowned. Angelique's knock on the door startled her.

"Okay if I come in?" Angelique asked awkwardly as she peeked her head in.

"Please, please," Catherine said as she quickly closed the desk drawers and rearranged her paperwork on the desk. "Thanks for being so patient. These things take time."

Angelique entered and sat down across from her. Her eyes had bags underneath them and her blonde hair was bundled up in a hair tie behind her head. A single blonde strand touched the side of her face as it stretched down to her collarbone. Angelique tucked it behind her left ear in an irritated fashion.

"Hi, Angelique. It's been a long day for you." Catherine folded her hands on the desk, giving Angelique all her attention.

"Yes. It *certainly* has been." Angelique shifted in the office chair, clearly uncomfortable.

"Did you get something to eat? The 7-Eleven across the street has okay sandwiches."

"That's what the other officer told me. Yes, I walked out for a bit and got a chicken mayo sandwich. Not bad. How long do I need to stay? May I leave after this and come back tomorrow?"

"Let's see how it goes. We have a few things to sort out. Quite a few loose ends at present. But I promise I will try. Do you have a place to stay here in Oliver? As you know, your home is still a sealed-off crime scene. It's off limits."

Angelique nodded. "Yes, of course. My parents still live in town. In fact, they are only a few blocks from the police station, on Bartlett Street. I'm going to stay with them till it is all over."

"Yes, you mentioned they were locals. And so as not to try your patience, I'll cut straight to the issue that has been most unclear to me. Pardon my directness."

"All good."

"Why exactly did you marry Sheldon?"

Angelique appeared perplexed. "I thought we covered that? I loved him, of course."

"Mmm. I believe that, but then, you also love Chris. So, start by telling me more about you and Sheldon. And let me be frank." She leaned onto her elbows with a comforting smile on her face. "I want the real nitty-gritty truth, because something seems a bit peculiar here. I don't really get what type of person he was or the nature of your relationship. I feel like it needs more clarification."

"I understand. At face value people often don't get what we had between us. Where should I start? Some of it is very personal, so I hope I don't get too emotional..." She checked her handbag for some tissue. "I guess it's better to simply get it over with." She took a deep breath and looked at ceiling for a moment. "When I was in nursing school, Sheldon Peterson was one of the sexiest ER docs at Foothills Hospital. He was fit, athletic, tall with great hair... very much a charming Richard Gere type. He had a reputation for being 'notoriously single' when I arrived. The George Clooney of Foothills ER. But hey, I was cute, too. I was a mere nursing student, but I know when eyes are on me, and I was in great shape. When we did our orientation walk-through, I caught his eye. The first time he saw me, the weight of his stare was right on my butt, and I played it. On one of my first days, as I was walking down the hospital hallway, I noticed him approaching out of the corner of my eye. He was heading toward the ER. Purposefully, I made an abrupt turn, causing him to 'accidentally' bump into me.

"He was very apologetic. I still recall the conversation. I said something like, 'Yeah, you have to be careful—I could've had urine or sharps in my hand.' To which he replied, 'Oh, you don't want to get poked on the first date?' I laughed, saying, 'First date?' He laughed too and said, 'No! I said first *day*, not date.' I teased him about it.

"He read the name on my uniform and blushed as my name rolled off his tongue. 'Angelique. Beautiful name.' The air was electric with desire. He looked me in the eyes, and after a pause that felt like a lifetime, he said, 'Let's do it, then. Let's obey that Freudian slip. Maybe it's destiny.' In his doctor voice, he asked formally, 'Nurse Angelique, would you please allow me, clumsy Sheldon, to take you on a *date*?' He scribbled his number on a prescription pad and asked me to send him my number.

"I did, of course. And Sheldon pulled up that next Friday evening in a shiny Lexus. We went to Caesar's, and the steak melted in our mouths. He was charming, funny, interesting, and such a sexy dresser. He literally swept me off my feet. The evening grew late, and the club scene opened up. We danced into the night. We laughed. We drank. We hung onto each other till we clung. And the night flowed into morning.

"And oh my goodness. The next morning, when I opened my eyes, I was completely confused and disoriented. I tried to figure out what and where I was. I touched the legs that lay across my lap, and the skin was soft and smooth. I brushed soft blonde hair off my face and realized it wasn't mine. I tilted my head to admire the beautiful blonde woman on the bed with me. Next to her, there was a guy who was way too gorgeous to be straight. And in his arms lay Sheldon. In the living room where we had fallen asleep, I was surrounded by sleeping, naked people on all the couches and the floor.

"I wanted to quickly sneak out of there, but as I reached around for my clothes, the room started to stir. Everybody suddenly seemed to realize that it was time to leave. I sat up and covered the essentials, but the others had way fewer inhibitions than I did. Naked people dug through the heap of clothing in the corner to find their own. My shock system was still recalibrating.

"Eventually, I was left sitting alone with Sheldon. He rolled over, and I almost drooled as his abs tightened up. He said, 'Good morning, angel,' in his deep, husky voice, and I knew I was in love.

"I thought I was the only one freaked out about the night's events, but he admitted that it was quite a unique experience for him too. The evening's events simultaneously intrigued me and freaked me out, because they were so far outside my comfort zone. We laughed about the strangeness of it all. Sheldon said I had met him at a very weird moment on his journey to find his true self and true love."

Angelique reached over and took a sip of water.

"Was it true love?" Catherine asked.

"Yes, I think so. We were like random partners on the same bus on a strangely similar journey. We started dating."

"Did you indulge in these... parties often?"

"Not often at all. Once in a while we'd do something exotic like that. These moments created such sensory and ecstatic overload that they overwhelmed us. The day after such a night, we would do nothing. We'd allow the sensations to filter out of us. No touching. No talking. No analyzing. Just *being*—allowing ourselves to settle and find peace and calm. I still remember that first morning, looking out of the big windows of his apartment on the thirtieth floor. As I curled into his arms on the couch, we watched the sun rise. The sun's rays painted the sky a golden hue, and when the first rays hit my skin, I felt the heat immediately. The world was intense. Nearly too intense. The percolating coffee smelled the best it ever had. I cuddled up to Sheldon, and he shielded me from the world. I will never forget his words: 'Hush, Angel. It's incredible, isn't it? So much beauty in this world... Sometimes it is too much, really.'"

Angelique's attention seemed to slowly return to the office after her reminiscence.

Catherine sat across from her and scribbled a few notes. She remained silent but then focused on Angelique.

Angelique was looking down at her hands. She adjusted her wedding band on her left ring finger, watching the reflections from the large diamond play in the light.

"You asked why I married Sheldon." Angelique said. "He allowed me to enter a world I had never known. I met a mind so free, it hypnotized me. I could go on a journey with him without even leaving the couch. I think I loved that part as much as I loved him."

Catherine nodded and smiled with understanding. "But..."

Angelique looked up. "Why do you think there needs to be a *but*?"

"There always is." Catherine made firm eye contact with Angelique. "Especially when that somebody ends up with a knife in their face. Seriously, do you truly want me to believe there wasn't a *but*?"

Angelique held her stare for the briefest of moments and then cast her eyes downward. "Okay, Catherine. You are right. Of course there was a *but*." She cleared her throat. "How do I explain it?" She rubbed her forehead. "When you are so free, so light, and flying so high, you can get to a point where you miss your roots. Other people, like Sheldon, are born with that inherent freedom and lightness and can live their entire lives in that fashion. I dreamed to be light and free, but my flight was short. Gravity was stronger. I flew for a while, but then my wings melted. I came down to earth like Icarus. My roots called. I needed to be grounded."

"I see." Catherine poured herself water from the jug at the far end of the desk, then looked toward Angelique. "Do you want some water?"

Angelique nodded. Catherine immediately handed her the glass she had just poured and then poured herself another. "How did you convince Sheldon to move from the exciting city hub to small-town Vaseux Lake, of all places?"

"Actually, it wasn't too hard. He had no roots. No family. And he burned a few bridges in Calgary. Years of burning the candle at both ends turned even the big city into a small town for him. He was getting older. He wanted a more peaceful setting. Calm lakeside mornings to do yoga on the dock. Mountain-bike rides with no one else around. A long-stride row with a calm glide in his kayak over a mirrored lake. You know, I sold him on the stuff city people always dream about. A peaceful mindfulness change. In truth, it came at the right time for us both."

"Did Chris play a role in this decision?"

"Yes, for sure. I knew he was having a tough time: he sounded extremely lonely, missing Mitch and missing me. He was desperate for me to come home. I reminded him that I was married and that it won't be the same as before. He said he didn't care; he just wanted me close. When the place on Sundial Drive came on the market, I begged Sheldon. He took a position in Oliver at the hospital but also got some ER sessions in Kelowna. You know, a bigger centre with teaching and so on."

"And Kelowna is a bigger city, with bigger-city

things..." Catherine nodded.

Angelique shot a sharp look at Catherine. "You don't miss a lot, do you?"

"That's why they pay me the big bucks." Catherine smiled.

"Yep. He would shoot off to Kelowna for a few days' locum once or twice a month. I asked no questions."

"Ask no questions, hear no lies."

"Maybe, but I don't know if you understand the type of freedom mindset that Sheldon lived in. It is something that I never really understood before I met him: a freedom to allow another to be himself without constricting him, without clinging to him, without being with him all the time, without sharing in all of his experiences, but allowing him to fly, knowing without a doubt that he will return and that he truly wanted to return. It was liberating to know that he enjoyed the flight of pleasure even more *because* he had a safe haven to return to. A place of peace and acceptance. A place of soulfulness to allow for the intensity to dissipate. Yet as liberating and progressive as it was initially, it did become very difficult for me at times. Clearly I was made of something different."

"Can I be honest with you?" Catherine leaned in with truth in her eyes.

"Of course," Angelique said.

"Very few couples are truly able to do that without things falling apart eventually. To love without attachment... I admire it. I even aspire to it at times in my own life, but it isn't easy."

"Thank you for saying that."

Catherine played with her necklace, and the light refracted green lines on the table. They both watched it spin.

"However…" Catherine dropped the word like a penny on a tiled floor.

"Yes?"

"Allowing this for him wasn't all altruistic, was it? It allowed you some of your own freedoms too."

Angelique shrugged.

Catherine looked at her sternly. "Cut the crap." A chilled silence filled the room. "I know all the philosophy about non-attachment, open relationships, and the intricacies associated with them. And I can tell you one thing: it only works if *both* parties benefit and enjoy the freedom *equally*." She leaned in close to Angelique. "I'm not buying what you are selling, Angelique. You were not prudishly sitting at home while Sheldon took flight. You allowed it for Sheldon because it gave you the freedom to have the affair with Chris, didn't it?"

Angelique took a deep breath and pursed her lips. She sat back and folded her arms.

Catherine put up her hand. "You know what, Angelique? You don't even have to answer. Your expression tells the whole story." She gathered her paperwork and put it in her folder. She got up from the chair and put the folder under her arm. "I need to talk to Chris about all of this. Why don't you get something to eat or drink? Have a coffee, reflect for a bit about where the truth really lies, and then come back to me. We can talk again a bit later."

Catherine slid the pregnancy test, wrapped in the evidence bag, across the table with her fingertips. "And we will get to this." She returned the evidence bag to her folder and left Angelique sitting in the office on her own.

Angelique slowly looked up and stared out the window, tissue in hand, dabbing at the tears running down her cheek.

15

"Hi, Chris. Sorry for making you wait. It's been tough getting to everybody. I appreciate your patience." Catherine placed a Tim Hortons coffee cup in front of him. "Got you a Timmy's dark roast. Hope that's okay? There's some sugar and cream." She handed him a small paper bag with the cup.

"Thank you. This is great." Chris added two sugars to the coffee and stirred. He attempted a smile. "Strange how we always say, 'Thank you for your patience.' But there is no real choice in the matter here, eh?"

"I agree. Life is strange that way."

"I was thinking about my life and everything that led me here, and then I looked at my situation from the perspective other people. I realized one thing as clear as day." He took a sip of the coffee. "I'm completely and utterly *fucked*."

"I disagree, actually. I think you have some options."

"Jesus, really?" Chris mumbled at his hands. "Catherine—is it okay if I call you Catherine?" She nodded. He continued. "Stop for a moment and look at my situation, would you? Although I tried to hide it, you figured out everything about me and Angelique. And I was found covered in her husband's blood, with his fucking dead body in front of me and a knife in his face! Any jury in the world would convict me. For fuck's sake, if I were a juror, *I* would convict me. Let's call it a day. Let's stop wasting everybody's time. I'm fucked no matter what I say. Why extend the torture? To be honest, my life was pretty screwed up anyway, so let me be. Okay?"

Catherine reached over the desk and touched his arm. She spoke in a soft, kind tone. "Chris, look at me."

He looked up.

"I know it might appear concerning, but Chris, allow me to say this: I honestly do not believe you killed Sheldon." She let it sink in and gave his arm a small squeeze before she sat back in her chair. "I am on *your* side here."

"Bullshit." He looked down at his hands wrapped around the coffee. The warmth soothed him. "It is so frustrating that I can't remember a thing about what happened. I guess it could be the stress, but no jury is going to believe that. And when I look at the facts of the situation, even *I* think that I must've done it. Why don't you? *Honestly.*"

"Two reasons. One"—she held up her right hand and extended her thumb—"there is proof that you tried to do CPR on him. Hence the blood on your hands. Why would you do that if you wanted him dead? Two"—she extended her index finger—"*you* were the one who dialled 911. So either you didn't stab him, or you are one of the stupidest murderers out there." She folded her hands and softened her tone even more. "Could you help me figure this out? I know it appears a bit grim, and you should probably get a lawyer for sure, but I promise you, I *do* have your best interests at heart, and I want to find the answers as certainly as you do. Do you believe me?"

Chris looked up. A tear shimmered in his eye. "Yes, I do."

"Okay, then. Let's figure this out together."

"Okay."

"Allow me to give you some background on what we are going to talk about. The way things play out always has a lot to do with the emotions that lie buried underneath it all. My questions might appear, at first glance, to be irrelevant to the actual case at hand, but I promise you, they all add up to give me the whole picture. Do you know where I'm coming from?"

"Yes."

"I spoke with Angelique, and she was completely unaware that you were admitted to the mental health unit when she flew to Mexico to get married. She knew nothing about your suicide attempt and was actually angry at you for years for not coming to the wedding. Why didn't you tell her the truth?"

"I didn't see the sense." Chris shrugged and looked away. "I know she would've wanted my blessing to marry him. However, by the time I heard her messages on my machine at home, she was married already. I couldn't change that, and if I told her then about my objections, it would only have made it worse! Clearly, I was no match for Dr. Sexy Gorgeous. She was obviously smitten. I'd be the whining asshole if I objected to my best friend marrying a beautiful, successful guy everybody loved. Who was I to keep her from that happiness? No way." Chris slowly got up and cautiously looked at Svenson. Svenson nodded, giving him the go-ahead. Chris stretched his spine in a backward arc. The crack of his vertebra was audible. "Ah, that felt so good." He sat back down. "No. I wasn't going to be the party-pooper, especially not after the fact. She needed to make that call for herself. Thank God I missed that phone call and had no opportunity to embarrass myself with an objection."

"I get that, but why not tell her about the suicide attempt?"

"Why? It would only be more embarrassing and make me look like an even bigger loser. And on top of that, it would've caused her a bunch of unnecessary concern. No, it was my personal stuff to deal with."

"After your admission to mental health, did they discharge you on medication?"

"Yes, they prescribed me some meds, and I took them for a while, but the drugs made everything bland, dull, and numb. I stopped them after a few months. T researched it, and he read that if I did physical exercise five times a week for thirty minutes to an hour, it could be as effective as the antidepressant. I also stopped the other meds..." He rubbed his forehead. "What were they called again? Something with a 'Q.'"

Catherine paged through her folder. "Your medical record has quetiapine listed."

"Yes! That's the one I was supposed to take at night for sleeping. Well, I stopped it because I was sleeping fine."

Catherine made a checkmark in her notes. "Okay. When you returned to the lake after the hospital stay, did things improve?"

"I don't know." He shrugged and pouted his lips. "I really missed Mitch, but it was more peaceful without Uncle George."

"Did you call Angelique a lot?"

"Once in a while."

"I guess you were happy when she decided to move back."

"Of course. I was ecstatic. Ian and T had their comments about it, but I was excited."

"What were the comments?"

"They kept reminding me that she was married and that things would not be the same as before she left. They knew I cared for her—but they were worried that things between us could fall apart. T said it could easily become a mess if we weren't careful. He was very concerned."

"A valid concern, with her being married and all."

"Exactly." Chris nodded decisively.

"But it worked out pretty well initially, it seems?"

"Yes. I knew it could. Ian and T were pleasantly surprised."

"Certainly appears that way." Catherine sat back in the chair. "All was good—until suddenly Sheldon got killed."

"You said it." Chris looked away at the mirror.

They sat in silence.

"And here we are, trying to figure out how a perfect situation could get so 'messed up' so quickly." Catherine tapped her pen on the table a few times. Then she interlinked her fingers and leaned in closer to Chris, looking him in the eye. "Do you want to know what I think messed it all up?"

"Of course!"

She slid the pregnancy test across the table for Chris to see. "When did you find out about Angelique's pregnancy?"

"Holy shit. What?" Chris yelled as he shot to his feet. His chair clanged across the floor. "Angelique is *pregnant*?"

Svenson lurched forward to protect Catherine from Chris's outburst. His left hand slammed onto Chris's chest, holding him back. His right hand was ready on the handle of his taser.

Chris was fuming. "What the fuck?" he hollered. "Why doesn't anybody tell me anything? Why didn't she tell me? Whose baby is it?"

"Back down! Sit down!" Svenson commanded.

16

Ian was pacing the room again. This was his distinctive behaviour when he was angry or worked up. Catherine sat by the table while Svenson stood right next to her, following Ian closely with his eyes and keeping himself partially between Ian and Catherine. Svenson was on high alert and would have preferred to subdue him, but Catherine had told him before, "Let him be; let him rant."

Ian glared at Catherine. "This is fucking ridiculous. Sure, question me and get your bloody answers, but I told you what I know: *nothing*. This is taking forever. I want to go home now."

Catherine didn't flinch at his outburst. She appeared calm and collected under fire. Ian took a slow breath and then sat down again.

"Ian," Catherine said in a calm, kind monotone, "I understand your frustration, and I sympathize. Unfortunately, these things take time, and the wheels turn slowly. Let's clear this up, and then we'll be closer to going home. Okay?"

"Fuck," he mumbled, and folded his arms. He stared at the mirror.

Catherine sat forward. Ian looked toward her. Her eyes mesmerized him. They pierced his soul, demanding the truth and unveiling any lies. Ian had never really noticed how intense they were.

He shook his head to refocus. "Okay. Whatever. Where were we?"

"We were talking about Angelique. I'm trying to piece together life at Vaseux Lake after Uncle George and Mitch died."

"What do you wanna know?"

"Tell me more about the suicide attempt."

"Chris was very depressed and lonely, missing Mitch and Angelique. I don't think he missed Uncle George since the guy was weird as fuck, but suddenly Chris was without any family. T and I were around, but it wasn't the same. Chris sat in the tree house for hours, looking over the lake. Then one day, out of the blue, he tried to hang himself." Ian rubbed his neck as he recalled the scene. "What is scary is that he would have been successful had it not been for the BC Hydro guy who arrived to review the scene of Uncle George's death. What a coincidence. That guy saved his life. He cut Chris down and called 911. Touch and go, or Chris would have been dead! Chris was admitted to the mental health unit. When he returned, he wasn't himself. He didn't want to hang out with me or T or anyone. That place drugged him until he was a zombie."

"A zombie?"

"Yes. T and I let him be for a while, but he clearly wasn't the Chris we knew. He didn't want to talk or even interact. The medicine, in my opinion, made him even unhappier. T was always researching stuff, and he knew a lot about medicine. It was he who convinced Chris to stop the evening medications. Those ones really knocked him out. Eventually, he quit everything. He wasn't back to normal, but at least we could talk again. He wasn't numb anymore."

"Did he miss Angelique?"

"Oh my God. Are you kidding me? He obsessed about her. He called her every single day. No lie. *Every* day. And if she didn't answer, he left these long messages on her answering machine."

"What would he say to her?"

"Basic stuff. I don't know... He'd talk about his day and what he did and how he missed her and how he was happy she was married but that he missed their friendship and how it was important to have roots. No roots, no flowers. On and on. Blah. Blah. Blah."

"Interesting..." Catherine said under her breath.

"What?"

"Oh. Sorry. It was just an interesting word choice: no roots, no flowers."

"Why?"

"Angelique used exactly the same terms."

"Of course."

"I guess his word seeds hit fertile soil. How did *you* feel about her moving to the lake?"

"I was of two minds about it. I'm not crazy about her —he sometimes shuts me out when she's around—but on the other hand... Meh. He was slowly coming apart at the seams without her. Sundial Drive is a lonely street. Vacation homes. People coming and going for weekends or holidays. We were the only permanent residents at the time. I liked the fact that there was no one else, but for Chris it was more difficult. And Angelique was his life-long friend. They had something special, I must admit.

Especially before she left for nursing school. For Chris's sake, I thought it would be great if she came back. I was a bit worried about Sheldon, though. Uncertain how that would influence things, you know?"

"Understandable. And how did it work out?"

"Surprisingly excellent, actually."

"Till Sheldon got stabbed."

"Of course. But it *did* go well for many years before the, um, incident."

"Did you and Sheldon get along?"

"I avoided him, but in fairness I mostly like to be left alone. Not a big 'people' person. I didn't mind Sheldon as long as he stayed out of my way, which he mostly did. It's a guy thing, I think. We didn't like each other, and it was a mutual understanding. He was more T's friend. Initially he tried to be all nice with me. But I wasn't into his nonsense, so when he came over, I'd just tell him that T wasn't in, so he could fuck off. That was that. Ground rules between us were established, and we got along. He hung out with T and let me be."

Catherine lifted her eyebrows, shrugged, and scribbled feverishly in her notebook as Ian continued.

"Anyway, Sheldon was a very narcissistic, self-involved guy—a self-proclaimed hedonist, all out to enjoy life. And that's what he did, in healthy and unhealthy ways. It was his life, so whatever."

"Healthy and unhealthy ways?"

"You know..."

She smiled kindly. "I might guess or presume to know, but I'd actually like you to tell me what you mean by that. Be specific. We all have different perspectives. I'd like to hear yours."

"I really like you. It's weird territory for me to like someone, but I like your no-bull attitude." Ian scratched his chin for a moment. "Specifics, she says... Healthy things like kayaking across the lake, sailing, swimming, and biking: road biking, mountain biking, and lately bikepacking. Unhealthy things like partying, drugs, dancing in nightclubs, and lots and lots of... sexual adventures. I was never sure which team he truly played for, if you know what I mean." Catherine acknowledged that. Ian folded his arms and sat back. "Honestly, I think he was more T's type: very good-looking. In fact, a little *too* good-looking." Ian lifted his arm off the table, let his wrist droop, and said jokingly in a higher tone, "What do I know? I was merely the neighbour.

"So you are insinuating that he was predominantly gay, and that got him killed."

Ian nodded, then shrugged. "I don't really care for his sexual preferences, but he was a douchebag and did not care about crossing moral lines. He pissed off many people, not only me." Ian stretched his legs. He walked back to table and leaned on the back of the chair, though he remained standing.

Svenson pointed to the chair.

"Mind if I remain standing?" Ian asked Svenson.

"Not at all," Catherine answered with a kind smile. "I have come to expect you to be up. You've been standing and pacing most of the time."

"I struggle to sit still."

"All good, as long as I can trust you not to hurt me."

"I would never hurt a lady."

"Thank you." Catherine's tone was soft, and she truly sounded appreciative. Ian nodded in response.

"Let's continue. Did T and Sheldon hang out often?"

"All the time. I don't know what happened behind closed doors, but their 'secret'"—Ian made air quotes —"was very obvious to me. Ask T. He and Sheldon were like this by the end." Ian twirled his index and middle fingers around each other. "They even went on an overnight bikepacking adventure the evening before it all happened. Who knows what they were up to on those trips?"

"And Angelique didn't mind?"

"I wouldn't know whether she *minded* or not, but she allowed it to happen without bitching about it. When he went on his 'locums' to Kelowna"—Ian made air quotes again—"Angelique stayed over with Chris in our house. I think the arrangement worked for both of them."

"You were neighbours. Did you ever hear them fight?"

"Sheldon and Angelique? Never. Well... except for last week."

Catherine looked up. "The evening he got killed?"

"I don't know. I wasn't there. I heard some noise. It could have been, but maybe it was a truck rumbling by on the highway."

"But you *did* admit that just a few nights ago—the night you had sex with Angelique—they'd also had a fight." Catherine paged through her notes.

"Well." Ian's eyebrows crumpled up. He started pacing. "To be honest, all I know with certainty about that night was that Angelique was very upset. Whether that was with Sheldon or more about Chris, I'm not sure. And I don't like to guess what was happening between Sheldon and Angelique; it was none of my business. You should ask her."

"Okay, Ian, I think we are nearly done." Catherine tapped the pen on her teeth again. It clearly annoyed Ian, because he fidgeted and shifted in the chair, staring at her mouth.

"Oh! One last thing."

"What?" he snapped. Even he appeared blindsided by his rude retort. "Sorry. I think I'm hungry."

She turned to Svenson. "Could you get Ian a sandwich or something to eat, please?"

Svenson looked at her for a few moments without moving.

"It'll be okay," she reassured him, and looked over at Ian. "Right?"

Ian nodded.

Svenson left reluctantly.

Catherine consulted her notes. "Chris was with Angelique from time to time, and T was with Sheldon behind the scenes, but it sounds like Sheldon was also philandering elsewhere."

"So?" Ian shrugged.

"A messy business, in my opinion, but everybody for themselves." Catherine tapped her teeth with the pen again.

"I actually agree. Messy it was. I held my breath, waiting for the wheels to come off any moment."

"I wonder, Ian: where did you fit in? Who were you into? What or who got *you* off?"

"Well, that is none of your fucking business, Catherine."

"Come on, Ian. I know it's personal, but there's no need to be rude. I think it's important to get the full picture."

"I am not into any of 'it,' as you say. By 'it,' do you mean sex? I have seen what sex does to people, and I don't like to get too close. I don't like that touchy-feely bullshit. It's all fake. Let Chris have it. Let T have it. I'll keep my eyes open, thank you very much. When others become starry-eyed and start making stupid, love-based decisions, I'm the one they can depend on to stay sensible. The one who does not fall into those traps. The one who's alert. The one who's looking out for trouble."

Catherine didn't look convinced. She pulled an awkward face, and Ian noticed her draw a question mark on her notepad. He flipped the chair around and sat down, leaning on the back rest with his arms.

Svenson returned, out of breath, with a standard-edition cafeteria sandwich wrapped in plastic. He gave it to Ian.

"Thanks." Ian looked at Svenson, immediately unwrapped it, and took a bite. He returned his attention to Catherine.

"Let me explain it this way. You know when kids in school want to be naughty—smoke or drink or have a bit of sex—and somebody has to stand by the door of the washroom to check that the teacher isn't coming? I'm that guy: the watchman. The one who prevents shit from hitting the fan. That is where I fit into 'it,' as you say." He got up again abruptly and walked away. "Somebody needed to protect Chris."

17

They were both staring at the pregnancy test.

Catherine was the first to speak. "So here we are, finally discussing the elephant in the room. You are pregnant, correct? This is yours?"

"Yes," Angelique replied.

"And I deduce that since we found it in your garbage, and garbage pickup was on Monday, you only recently did this test... around Tuesday this week."

"Yes."

"After years of peaceful acceptance of all the sneaking around, suddenly there is chaos on Sundial Drive. I ask myself why. Coincidence? No way. On Tuesday, you found out you were pregnant, and the very same day you had your first big fight with Sheldon in years. I think this little test must've had something to do with it all. Don't you?"

"Maybe." Angelique shrugged, trying hard to appear calm.

Catherine pulled a piece of paper from the folder and placed it in front of her. The cover sheet read *Dr. Sheldon Peterson. Preliminary autopsy report.*

Catherine continued. "These reports often contain a ton of boring facts: things the pathologist writes for the sake of completeness, thinking they have no relevance to the case. But a tiny detail can make all the difference because of the context. Do you know what that little detail might have been in the case of your husband, Sheldon?"

"No," Angelique said softly.

"Tsk. Come on, at least read it. I am sure you can guess."

Angelique shrugged.

"Ugh. You're no fun," Catherine said lightly—but the undertone was firm. She dramatically turned the pages of the report to find the item she was looking for. It was marked with a sticky arrow tag. She rotated the folder and tapped on the appropriate place. "Read that out loud, please."

Angelique read, "Previous surgeries and surgical scars: appendectomy, cholecystectomy, arthroscopy left and right knee. ACL repair right knee. UCL repair left thumb. Vasectomy—" She paused.

"Yes, *indeed*." Catherine read her mind. "Vasectomy. Can I tell you my theory about this?"

Angelique quietly stared at her.

"I think he never told you. I think Sheldon kept that gem of a detail hidden from you. You know why I think so?"

Angelique seemed numb.

"I think any young, beautiful woman marrying a heartthrob like him contemplates, at least for a split second, 'I wonder how beautiful our kids would be?'"

"Not true. I told him I didn't want kids."

"That may have been true initially, but then time goes by, and you are not twenty-one anymore, and a clock starts ticking somewhere inside your head. You're not in the party scene anymore... Do you see what I am getting at?"

Angelique conceded with a little nod.

"One day, out of the blue, let's imagine"—Catherine paused for dramatic effect—"a kid falls and cries in the supermarket and runs into the arms of his mother. She hugs him and kisses the boo-boo better, and you stop in your tracks and say to yourself, 'Holy shit, I want one of those.' Sound familiar?"

Angelique remained silent.

"Nothing?" Catherine smirked. "When did you start volunteering at the child-care centre?"

"Last year," she mumbled as she looked at the floor.

"When you met Sheldon, did you guys talk about kids?"

"We touched on it. I didn't want any at that stage, and I knew he was older. He sort of joked and tiptoed around it. You know, saying things like, 'Geez, I don't think so, but you never know. They are cute sometimes, but then they cry, and poof, the cuteness is gone like that!' And he'd snap his fingers. Or, 'I don't know about kids. Everybody say it's the best thing ever, but then they complain about not having enough fun, time, or money.' Sheldon's opinion was that the 'pleasure' of kids was Mother Nature's biggest con on humans to trick them into procreating. He made lots of comments like that. We let it be. We stopped talking about it."

"I presume that you didn't know he got a vasectomy."

Angelique shook her head.

"When did you finally find out?"

Angelique squirmed in her chair.

"Angelique... please answer."

"I found out three days ago."

"That's what I thought! I guess he dropped that titbit of information on you when you told him that you were pregnant."

"Yes! How did you know?"

"Not my first rodeo." Catherine smiled kindly. "What a shocker that must've been."

"I was furious. He could've told me before. We were very open about everything. I was mad that he'd kept it a secret. And he was such an ass about it, too."

"How did the conversation play out?"

"Well, we had discussed kids before, but when this unplanned pregnancy arrived, I suddenly felt differently. I was hoping he'd understand. I can't really recall the play-by-play, but I approached it cautiously. I told him a story about this sweet little kid at daycare who ranted about how much he loved his dad for taking him out on the lake to go fishing. He was so cute, and he drew a picture of a big fish that he'd caught. I told Sheldon I was having second thoughts about not having kids and wanted to revisit the issue.

"Initially he said, 'I don't think so.' But then he became blatantly rude by saying things like, '*No* fucking way. That ship has sailed.' My world collapsed, so I blurted out that I was pregnant. He said, 'Well, it ain't fucking mine! When last did we have sex? Go talk to your fucking boyfriend about that.' I told him that it could be his, after all, and he said, 'Impossible!' He made a scissoring motion in the air. 'I've had the snip-snip!'

"I exploded. We had this huge blowout, and he told me he'd had it done about a year ago, when I—and I remember these words specifically—'became all googly-eyed for every kid at the daycare.' Such an asshole! I was furious, so I stormed out to tell Chris next door."

"But you didn't tell Chris, right?"

"I wanted to." Angelique paused. "But no, I didn't. He doesn't know yet."

Catherine looked down at her hands for a moment. "Angelique, I owe you an apology." She cleared her throat. "I accidentally revealed that to Chris today. I—"

"You told him? What the fuck? What about confidentiality and all that shit?"

"I'm truly sorry. Honestly, I thought he knew already..." Catherine reached over to touch Angelique's hand, but Angelique pulled away and got up. She turned her back to Catherine and walked to the window.

"Fuck," Angelique whispered. "How did he take it?" She sniffed and reach for a tissue.

"He was truly shocked. I mentioned it because I thought it might have been his motive for stabbing Sheldon, but I was completely wrong." Catherine walked around the desk to Angelique. "But his response supports his defence at least. The pregnancy was not a motive because he obviously didn't know at the time."

"So you think Chris might be innocent?"

"We're still figuring it out. Unfortunately, the case is more complicated than we expected."

They both slowly returned to their seats.

Catherine checked through her notebook. "Let's recap. You had your big fight with Sheldon about your pregnancy and his vasectomy on Tuesday night. Sheldon left the next morning to go bikepacking, stayed out Wednesday night on his two-day trip, and returned yesterday morning—Thursday."

Angelique nodded confirmation.

"And then on Thursday night, last night, he got stabbed."

Angelique nodded again.

"When the police arrived at the scene, they initially

could not find you. But eventually they found you sitting in the tree house by the lake. Why were you there?"

"I needed to get fresh air."

"Why? When did you go there? After the incident?"

"No! Before. I was in the tree house the whole time. I guess I'm lucky. If I had been in the house, I could've been stabbed too."

"Getting fresh air..." Catherine said very slowly. "Why? People say that when they are angry and need to step out and cool down. Did you have another fight with Sheldon?"

Angelique sighed and put her head in her hands. "We never used to fight before."

"Was it about the same thing? The pregnancy?"

"Sort of... I can't recall it all. Maybe it's the hormones?"

Catherine stared long and hard at Angelique. Then she pulled more papers out of the folder and pulled her chair closer to the table.

"We found a fresh drop of Sheldon's blood in the tree house." She pointed to a photograph of the blood droplet. "We found a print, partially caked in Sheldon's blood, on the handle of the knife. They told me, just now, that the print matches you."

"Fuck," Angelique mouthed silently as she looked down.

"This does not look good for you, Angelique. Only the truth will suffice."

"I did not kill Sheldon."

"Maybe."

After a long pause, Catherine spoke as if she could read Angelique's mind. "Angelique, the evidence is putting you in a very tight spot. If you want me to believe that you didn't kill Sheldon, then it is time to tell me exactly how it all played out. That is the only hope you have. The evidence against you is very damning. Tell me every detail. *Ev-er-y* detail, okay? I need to know why your fingerprints are on the murder weapon, how his blood ended up in the tree house, where the police found you..."

Angelique nodded. Her hands were tremoring, so she laced her fingers and put her hands in her lap.

"Start with where you were in the afternoon, before the murder," Catherine said in a reassuring tone.

Angelique closed her eyes for a moment. "Late afternoon is the best time of the day at Vaseux Lake. The sun dips behind the mountain in the west, and the cliff side throws a tall shadow over the lake. Even on a windy day, the breeze has an eerie tendency to calm down at dusk. It is certainly the most peaceful time of the day. My ritual was to spend forty-five minutes doing yoga on the dock every day at sunset. Sheldon sometimes took his C1 canoe out at the same time, especially when the lake became a mirror. I don't know if you are aware of this, but he was an excellent canoer, having competed in the sport in Victoria in his youth. He loved the glide.

"The lake was exceptional when I started my yoga session on the dock. I knew Sheldon was back from the bikepacking trip because I'd seen his biking gear spread out by the shed. He always washed everything after a trip and hung it up to dry in the sun. I tried to meditate, but found it odd that Sheldon wasn't coming out for a row on an obviously perfect day for it. I wondered if he was avoiding me or something. I tried my utmost to let it be, but my mind would not settle, maybe because of our recent fight. Besides, I needed to pee. Lately I have been peeing so frequently; it's probably the pregnancy, or anxiety—who knows. Between my thoughts festering over Sheldon and my bladder bugging me, my meditational yoga was simply ruined. After fifteen minutes, I gave up and ran into the house to use the bathroom.

"As I stormed in through the kitchen back door, I had a straight view of Sheldon's study. In the house, we respected each other spaces. He had his study, which I rarely entered. And I used one of the upstairs bedrooms, which had a great view of the lake, for my painting and photography studio.

"I don't know why it irked me, but as I entered the house, the door of his study drew to a close in a peculiar way. Something was visually odd about it. Usually when I entered the house through the back door, the burst of air pushed Sheldon's study door open a little wider. Instead, this time, it moved toward me, as if he'd closed it intentionally. I immediately suspected something sinister was going on in the study. I was emotional, hormonal, and still upset about our recent fight. All of this caused me to sprint down the hallway and burst into Sheldon's office without knocking.

"I caught him dick in hand. Buck naked. Red-handed, as they say. He was watching porn on the large screen in his study and jerking off like a madman. His penis was still hard, pulsating and oozing onto his hand. It was dirty, cheap, and it disgusted me to the core.

"I can't remember what I yelled, but it was something like, 'Perv! Fucking asshole! It's a gorgeous day outside, and here you are in a dungeon jerking off!' I stormed out and slammed the study door. Sheldon despised a slamming door. I knew this. He chased after me and caught me in the kitchen. 'What the fuck is wrong with you?' he hollered.

"I think we were both on edge because of the pregnancy thing. It ripped open the fact that we did have secrets, that we had lied to each other. We based our marriage on being completely open about everything—our desire for each other but also for others. 'Brutal honesty' was our motto. Suddenly this 'little' secret was a big thing. It pointed a distrusting finger at the foundation of our relationship. We both struggled with it."

Angelique shrugged and took a sip of water from the glass on the table. "Anyway, that is my explanation for what happened next, because we had never yelled at each other like that. It was horrible. We were both blind with anger, and we spewed it at each other with no filter.

"During this fight, I turned my back on Sheldon at some point. He grabbed me violently from behind and swung me around, screaming, 'Don't you fucking turn your back on me, woman.' On the countertop was a knife I had left there earlier after cutting my fruit. As he swung me around, I grabbed it out of instinct and slashed at him in a rage. He reflexively jumped out of the way. It was a lucky miss, for the knife was surely heading straight for his chest. 'Jesus!' he yelled. I started shaking when I realized what I could have done.

"Then I saw the blood pouring from his hand. The blade had caught the palm of his defensive hand. He applied pressure to stop it. He said, 'Fuck, Angelique, you could've killed me.' Ironically, those were his last words to me. What a strange world we live in. He turned and walked to the bathroom.

"My insanity evaporated. I dropped the knife on the countertop and ran toward the tree house. I yelled that I was sorry as I left. I washed my hands in the lake and climbed up into the tree house, where I cried my heart out. I sat there all night, smoking a few joints and trying to make sense of my life. That's where the police found me later and broke the news that Sheldon had been murdered.

"I did not kill Sheldon. I only cut his hand. Honest to God, that is all. I did not stab him in the face! He was fine when I ran out. You have got to believe me. Please."

Catherine squinted. She touched her chin and said, "Maybe. Maybe most of it. You two were screaming and hollering, and it was a quiet, calm evening by the lake, right?"

"Yes."

"All the sliding doors at the front of the house were open when we found Sheldon. Was it that way while you had the fight?"

Angelique shrugged. "I did not open or close those, and I entered through the side kitchen back door when I came into the house. What does this have to do with anything?"

"Just answer the questions, please. Every detail is important. Which way did you leave when you ran out?"

Angelique contemplated the question. "I left through the open sliding door. You're right. They must've all been open all along."

"Thank you." Catherine made a note. "That will be all for now, Angelique."

Angelique's face scrunched up. She stood awkwardly. "That sounded very formal... too fucking formal. Did I say something wrong, Catherine?"

"Angelique, thank you for your co-operation. Could you please return to the waiting area? Do not leave the station till I get back to you." Her eyes were ice cold.

"Am I under arrest?" Angelique grew more frantic. "Should I call a lawyer?"

Catherine briefly glanced at Svenson. "You are not

under arrest yet, but I advise you to consider a lawyer at this point."

Angelique swayed on her feet. She found her balance by holding onto the desk for a moment. She gathered herself, straightened, and walked out the office. In the hallway, she took her phone out of her handbag.

18

S venson closed the door and lifted his hand for a high five. Catherine smiled and high-fived him, but it was a half-hearted slap.

"Fuck, Catherine. That was amazing. You got her. Of course, she wouldn't admit to everything yet, but she admitted to enough to nail her. Circumstantial will take us all the way. A jury would convict for sure. Who's going to believe that she fought, yelled, and screamed only to cut the guy's hand? Are you kidding me? She had the upper hand and the murder weapon. No jury's going to believe that she turned and ran away at the very last moment." He slumped into the chair.

"Sorry to burst your bubble, Svenson, but I think she's talking truth. I don't think she stabbed him in the face."

"Are you fucking kidding me? You're buying that bullshit?"

"Listen, I know we're close." Catherine opened the file and took out the pictures. "But look. The cut on his hand is a clean cut. A linear slash. A line. Like when you swing the knife through the air. She did not stab at him. She cut him as she swung it, like she said."

"And then she fucking stabbed him in the face and ran!"

"No. Look at the crime scene picture. See the blood pattern on the countertop there? That's where she put down the knife. Look at the shape. It's the handle. But most importantly, if she killed him in a fit of passion, why was there blood on the toilet roll in the bathroom? And why did Sheldon have tissue in the palm of his hand?"

Svenson dropped his head. "Fuck."

"Yeah. 'Fuck' is the scientific term for that, isn't it? He must've been well enough to walk to the bathroom, grab toilet paper, and compress the bleeder. Someone else came afterward to stab him to death. The knife was on the kitchen counter, and the doors were open. Problem is, it could've have been anybody. Even a random stranger since, all the doors were open. To be honest, I'm a bit worried that we have narrowed our scope too much. We might have missed some outlier."

"Shit."

"I think we've made great progress, but we must be careful not to jump to conclusions. Let's review what we have."

Svenson left the office and came back with a stack of folders. He sat down. "Okay. I'll go through each of the folders as I assigned them to the team."

Catherine pulled out her notepad.

"The dating sites. Sheldon was very active on Grindr and Tinder. He mostly had hookups with people travelling through, but he had a few repeat dates in Kelowna, and there were two people in Oliver he saw a lot more frequently."

"Interesting. Guys or gals?"

"The two in Oliver are actually a couple. From his phone records and text messages, it appears that he visited them regularly. JC and Samantha. Even more interesting, lately Sheldon had been making individual contact with JC. He texted 'no sam' in one of the messages, and then a drool-face emoji and a peach." Svenson seemed to notice something on the phone records in front of him. "Hmm, that's interesting..." He paged back through the folder. "Catherine, what is the presumed time of death?"

"The 911 call was 8:42pm, so a few minutes before that."

"And what time was sunset?"

"Sunset was 7:21 p.m.," Catherine said, confirming with the weather channel on the computer.

"If Angelique did her dusk yoga just prior to the fight, then their altercation must've been between 7:30 and 8:00 p.m., I guess. Right?"

"Yes, why?" Catherine leaned over to check what Svenson was looking at.

"Look here." Svenson pointed to a specific billing line. "Sheldon called JC on his cell phone at 8:17 p.m. They spoke for thirty seconds. What do you think that was about?"

He pulled the phone closer and dialled.

"Hello, this is JC."

Svenson pressed the speakerphone button. Catherine sat back and listened.

"Good evening, JC. This is Officer Svenson from the RCMP here in Oliver. Do you have a moment?"

"Um, yes, Officer. I will step out for a second. The ER is pretty busy, though. How can I help?"

"You work in the ER?"

"Yes. I'm an emergency physician. I presume this is something about Sheldon?"

"Yes. I'm sorry to bother you. We might need to set up a formal statement, but I have a quick question or two. Last night, according to telephone records, Sheldon called you at 8:17 p.m. You were the last person he spoke to."

"Really? That is, excluding the person who murdered him, obviously. And I swear that wasn't me. Jesus."

"Okay, point taken. I sense you are nervous. Can you please tell me why he called you?"

"He said he'd had an accident and cut his hand. He needed stiches. He wanted to know if we were busy in the ER. I told him we were, but that he could pop over anytime. He said he'd call back later when it was quieter. I offered to visit after my shift and stitch up his hand. He thanked me and said that would be great. That was it."

"And did you go out there as you said?"

"Yes, I did. My shift ended at eleven, and I grabbed a suture tray and drove out there. When I arrived, RCMP vehicles were everywhere, and you guys had sealed off the whole street. One of the officers told me I should go home. They took my name and said they would be in touch. I was expecting your call."

Svenson clenched his jaw, frustrated by the failure of his colleagues to follow through. "Thank you, JC. One more thing. You and your wife Samantha knew Sheldon socially. Or rather, um, intimately. Correct?"

JC replied in a low, cautious tone, "Yes."

"But lately it appears from your texts that you saw Sheldon on your own a few times."

JC cleared his throat. "Yes?" he whispered.

"Did that cause any issues at home? Was Samantha okay with that?"

The line went silent for a long time. "That is extremely personal, Officer."

"I understand, but so is murder. Could you answer me, please?"

"Sam doesn't know," he mumbled over the line.

"Okay. Thank you. Can you call the main desk at our office tomorrow and set up a formal statement to confirm these details, please?"

"For sure."

"Thank you for your help, JC. We'll speak to you soon."

"You're welcome."

Svenson ended the call. "Bi now, gay later, you said?"

Catherine nodded.

"Enough motive?"

"Keep him in mind. See if you can track his activities that night. Sounds like he might have a strong alibi, as he said he was working in the ER till eleven. And the gay relationship was a relatively new development. I don't really see the opportunity or motive for him to drive out there to murder Sheldon."

"People have killed for less."

"Maybe, but the timelines don't work. We can check his alibi, but I think it'll be solid. Any other options?"

"We did find a few pissed-off Grindr hookups who were stupid enough to fall in love with him. I'll let the guys filter through them. Most were transient from what I can see, and there are one or two who live in Kelowna." Svenson shook his head as he reviewed the folder. "Whew. Sheldon was quite the charmer and player."

"Seems like it."

Svenson pushed the social media folder aside. "Okay. We'll get back to that. Nothing earth-shattering there." He opened the next one.

After he scanned the contents, he said, "Seems like Sheldon did stir things up in Calgary." Svenson slid the folder over to Catherine. "He took out a restraining order against this guy, Dr. O'Brien, after O'Brien punched him —allegedly because he slept with O'Brien's wife. To pour oil on the fire, it appears O'Brien is the chief of staff at Foothills. Sheldon's superior."

"That provides extra clarity on why Sheldon was eager to leave Calgary. However they left Calgary 10 years ago. Why would that be relevant? How far is Calgary from Vaseux Lake, anyway?"

"Phew." Svenson shrugged. "Eight hours' drive minimum, I guess. I agree it is a long shot, but it is relevant. Dr. O'Brien recently got divorced."

"From the cheating wife?"

Svenson nodded. "Looks like it. That certainly might be motive, if he blamed Sheldon for the marriage demise."

"Agree. Let someone have a chat with Dr. O'Brien."

Svenson took the folder back, wrote a note on the inside sleeve for the investigating officer, and closed it.

As he read the next folder, he abruptly said, "This is *very* interesting. Come with me!" Svenson walked out, and Catherine followed.

"What?"

Svenson winked at Catherine. "I don't want to spoil the suspense."

He walked into an office where a nerdy officer was glancing between two computer monitors. "Paul, this is Catherine. Catherine, Paul." They both nodded.

"Paul, can we have a look?" Svenson asked.

"Svenson, what is it?" Catherine asked impatiently.

Svenson smiled at her. "Paul is our IT guy. He discovered that Sheldon had Chris's house bugged with spy cameras. Paul found a ton of digital video footage on Sheldon's computer hard drive. A *ton*. He is now working through it and documenting all the files and scenes."

Svenson smiled and looked at Paul. "Tough job, hey, Paul?" He slapped Paul on the shoulder, and the young officer blushed. On his screen, Chris and Angelique were having sex in what looked like Chris's bedroom.

Catherine glanced at the screen. "Where are the cameras located?"

"Here." Paul picked up a plastic evidence bag with a tiny black square in it. "We retrieved these from all over the house. They are so tiny, nobody would notice them. The victim had it all linked up through the Internet. He used his own Wi-Fi network. He merely installed a strong beacon in his place, and since they were neighbours, it all linked up. Sneaky clever."

"Anything useful in the video footage?"

"Depends on your perspective. Lots of sex, of course. Sheldon also had another folder called *Trio*. Most of those files contain conversations in the house."

"What are those about?"

"Mostly arguments about Angelique, from the bit that I have seen. And then he had this folder filled with security camera footage."

"True Big-Brother voyeurism, hey, Paul?"

"Sheldon was a creep for sure."

"Anyway, this is amazing evidence. Can you see from the computer viewing history which file he viewed or accessed last?"

"Yes." Paul did a quick search. "Found it."

Paul pressed play. The scene was Chris's kitchen. It was violent sex. Angelique was bent over the counter, being choked around the neck from behind. Through the partial choke, she yelled out, "Fuck me! Harder. Harder.

Harder. Fuck me." The man's face wasn't visible from the angle of the camera.

Catherine turned to Svenson. "I suspected Angelique was hiding some detail when she told her story about Sheldon masturbating; she seemed awkward. *This* is what she was lying about. She wouldn't get so angry about normal porn and jerking off. But she walked in on him jerking off to this voyeuristic porn tape—with *her* in it."

Svenson leaned toward the monitor for a closer look. He tilted his head. "Think it's Ian she's having sex with?"

"I think so, judging by the anger of the sex." She turned to Paul. "Please confirm the exact time that clip was last viewed."

"Thursday. 7:38pm. "

Catherine nodded. "Great job. Please, Paul, I need the Trio folder. I'll watch it later—those conversations will be very informative. Have you watched the security footage?"

"That's a bit peculiar. It looks like footage digitized from old video dating back to the house's previous owners. Even before Sheldon moved in. It's poor quality. Just hours and hours of footage of mind-numbing surveillance. Augh."

"Why would he have that?"

"I don't know, but I'll work through it once I get all the sex tapes sorted."

"Great job, Paul. Keep us posted."

Catherine and Svenson returned to the office.

"That was ground-breaking work," Catherine said. "Congratulate the team next time, please. Anything else?"

Svenson looked through the other folders. "Maybe this one. It's the BC Hydro investigation into the death of George Williams—Uncle George."

"And?"

"Deemed an act of God. Freak accident. Not much in it. The officer got the number for the investigator and the BC Hydro linesman for that area. He spoke with the investigator. Nothing new there. Electrocution after a high-power line was knocked down onto the zip line. He tried to call the linesman for the area, but he wasn't available."

Catherine leaned back in thought. "Could you hand me that number? I want to give it another try."

She dialled the number. It rang for a long time and then: "Hello?"

Her face lit up. "Hello. Is this Matthew Sheppard?"

"Yes. Who is this, again?"

"Sorry to bother. I'm Catherine McBride. I'm part of the investigation team at the RCMP. We are looking into an incident here in Oliver. We understand you were the linesman for BC Hydro at Vaseux Lake?"

"RCMP? Wow. Yes, I worked there for many years. Only moved away six months ago. I spoke with someone else before, I think?"

"Thank you for speaking to us—this won't take long. Do you recall the property at the end of Sundial Drive on Vaseux Lake?"

"Of course! That's where that old guy got electrocuted, isn't it?"

"Yes."

"Wait. Did somebody get electrocuted again?"

"No. You can relax. But what do you recall about this incident?"

"Not much. Freak thing. High-power line fell on the zip line. Old guy grounded the zip line. Boom. Done."

"Anything strange about the incident?"

"Not really. I still recall the geeky boy who lived with

him, though. Very inquisitive kid. He was always asking me tons of questions about high-power lines and insulators. Usually teenagers don't give a hell about my job, but this kid was like a shadow. Almost irritatingly so. A shadow that never stopped asking questions every time I did my meter readings."

"Thank you. That was very helpful. Anything else you recall about the property?"

"Oh my God—the hanging! How could I ever forget that? I swear that place is haunted. I was the one who found the kid who had hung himself there. I cut him down myself."

"Did you recognize him as the 'shadow' kid who asked you the questions before?"

"Not really. After the hanging, his face was all swollen and blue. Ugh. His tongue was enormous and sticking out of his mouth like a lizard. I thought he was dead. Geez. I had nightmares for a long time after that incident. We never see stuff like that in my line of work."

"Well, it's lucky you were sent out that day to check out the accident scene, isn't it? He would have been dead if it weren't for that."

"Accident scene? No. I wasn't there for the accident investigation. That made it even stranger. I was there for a prank call."

Catherine paused. "Oh? What happened?"

"Someone called the BC Hydro emergency line and said they'd seen sparks on a conductor of the power line at the end of Sundial. I rushed out there because BC Hydro gets a massively bad rap if our lines cause any forest fires. It was midsummer and super dry. When I got there, there were no sparks. But I took a look around and saw the kid hanging from a tree."

"Did they ever figure out who called?"

"No, I don't think they ever did. Maybe a vehicle driving by on the highway?"

Catherine made a note.

"Strange, though. That's all I can say."

"No doubt. Thank you." Catherine hung up and looked at Svenson. "What do you make of that?"

"Fuck. It gets weirder and weirder." Svenson rubbed his forehead.

"Really? I think it is all falling into place." Catherine smiled. "Let's go talk to Ian."

19

Catherine seemed to be in bit of a hurry. She was rushed and clumsy.

She dropped her thick folder and notebook on the table. Her pen rolled off, and as she dived to catch it, she bumped over the glass of water. It spilled all over the desk and into Ian's lap. Ian jumped up.

"So sorry!" She grabbed the folder again to prevent it from getting wet. After drying the mess with some paper towel and handing Ian some paper towels to dry himself, she sat down. "Oh my goodness, how clumsy am I? Truly sorry about that."

Ian was fuming. He paced as he tried to dry his pants with the paper towels.

"Whatever," he snapped.

She took a deep breath. "Can I hand you more paper towels?"

"I truly don't care about wet pants, okay? Can I go home now?"

Catherine cleared her throat.

"We are making great progress. I don't need to ask you

too much. I think we are honestly about to wrap this up. How does that sound?"

"Fucking great! I am still hungry." He looked at Svenson. "That tiny sandwich is long gone. Do you starve me intentionally to keep me pissed off?"

"Maybe." She laughed. "No, of course not." Her expression sobered. She opened her folder to the spot she was looking for. She wrote down Ian's name and the date and time. She carefully placed her pen at the top of her pad and folded her hands as she looked Ian straight in the eye. "I think I know who murdered Sheldon, and I thought you should know."

"Really? Who?"

"Angelique."

"What?" Ian squawked. He cleared his throat and poured some water into the glass. After a sip, he said, "No fucking way. Really?"

"You okay?" she said. "You look pale. Have some more water."

"Um. Bit of a shock." His forehead showed beads of sweat, and he grabbed a paper towel to wipe his brow as he spoke. "Why on earth would you think she did it?"

"Well, all the evidence stacks up that way. Chris clearly didn't do it; he was truly trying to help Sheldon. He got blamed for the death in error; purely circumstantial and no motive. In contrast, Angelique had all the motive. She was angry at Sheldon for lying to her. She was pregnant with Chris's baby, and Sheldon did not want kids—"

"What? Angelique is pregnant?"

"Yes." Catherine paused to let it sink in. "And to crown it all, Sheldon had had a vasectomy that she wasn't aware of. Her pregnancy announcement to Sheldon turned into a confirmation of her affair with Chris."

"Oh my God."

"That led to two big, emotional fights, and the last one got out of hand. Lots of anger. And lots of evidence."

"Evidence?"

"Yes. Her prints were on the murder weapon, and Sheldon's blood was found in the tree house with Angelique. Slam dunk. Case closed." Catherine made a hand-washing motion and started packing up her stuff. "I thank you for your co-operation, Ian. You were very patient with us. You can get something more to eat now..."

"Fuck." Ian slumped down in the chair but shifted around uncomfortably. He looked at the floor as he bounced his knee. "Fuck," he said again, and rubbed the back of his head vigorously. He swallowed hard and took another sip of water.

"Everything okay, Ian? As I say, you are free to leave. We have our murderer."

"Angelique is pregnant with Chris's baby, and now she's going to jail? Oh my God. Chris will be devastated." Ian nibbled on the nail of his index finger. "Fuck."

"What is it?" Catherine asked.

"Um. Um. Fuck. It is not right. I can't let that happen. I can't stand for such an injustice."

"What do you mean, Ian?"

"It wasn't Angelique. She's innocent."

"I know it seems strange, but I'm quite sure about this. Murderers come in all shapes and sizes. I know it seems unbelievable, but the evidence is overwhelming. She is going to jail for a long time—"

"No, no, no. Can't let that happen. It was me. I did it."

"What?"

"Is the video recorder on?" Ian said.

Catherine nodded and pointed to the flashing red light of the camera in the top corner of the room.

Ian got up and walked over to face the camera directly. "I hereby admit to stabbing Dr. Sheldon Peterson in the face with a knife and killing him." He turned and sat down again.

Catherine nodded slowly. After a long, quiet pause, she said, "I am so glad you came around to telling us the truth, Ian. I suspected you had that sort of honour in you. I knew you wouldn't let anybody else take your blame. I truly respect a man that can assume responsibility for what he did." She reached out and touched his arm. "Really. I respect that in you."

"Thanks."

"I have my own theories, but could you tell the camera why you did it? It would be good for you psychologically to release that burden. It would be a cleanse. A purification."

He cleared his throat and drank some more water. "Can I start by saying that I never intended for things to go this way? It all spiralled out of control so quickly."

"I think we all realize that."

Ian scratched his head and leaned back in the chair. "Ugh! I can't change the way things are. But it started with the fight between Sheldon and Angelique on Tuesday, which resulted in Angelique being upset and angry and storming over to our place. She didn't tell me what that fight was about. I honestly didn't know it was because she was pregnant. Her emotions were a mix of anger and lust, and it got wild. We had sex, and I know we shouldn't have. So on Wednesday, I stayed under the radar. I can't even recall what I did, but on Thursday after sunset, I heard them fighting again. It was only their second fight in, like, ten years of marriage, and it was merely two days after the first one. It made me nervous. Something was gonna give. Honestly, they'd never even yelled at each other before. We did the yelling in our house, but not Angelique and Sheldon. It unnerved me. I knew the Chris-and-Angelique and T-and-Sheldon situations were very meticulously balanced, intricate and fragile, so I feared things were unravelling. I also predicted that if the balance destabilized, everything would fall apart. I felt like the watchman again. Trouble was coming. Shit was going to hit the fan.

"I was outside Thursday evening. The lake was exceptional. No breeze at all. The reflection was so pristine you could flip the world upside down and it would look the same. The lake was the sky, and vice versa. For a moment, I was hypnotized by the peace and beauty. And then, like shattering a mirror, Angelique and Sheldon's fighting destroyed the tranquility. The sounds of violence, drama, and hate rolled out of their house and across the lake. The loons floating stirred into abrupt flight, causing the mirrored image to disappear under the ripples.

"I will never forget the sight of Angelique running from the house. Her waving blonde hair. Tears pouring from her eyes and down her cheeks. The peaceful life we had was fractured. I looked at her as she ran past me, and I knew I needed to fix it. I decided to go talk to Sheldon.

"I walked in as Sheldon was washing his bleeding hand in the washroom sink. When he came out, he was still mad, pressing tissue on the wound.

"'What the fuck do you want?' he snapped at me. 'Go mind your own fucking business, you crazy fuck!'

"I tried to calm him down, but he was livid. I had never seen him like that. He was pacing to and fro, even though he was butt-naked. He was sweaty, clammy, and taking deep breaths. He looked like he was having a panic attack or something. His face was red, and the veins in his neck were engorged with blood. He was a mix of fear and anger. Something was seriously wrong with him, and I tried to talk him down. I asked him what was going on, trying to settle things. Then he snapped.

"He stormed at me. He shoved his face right up to mine and hollered at top volume, '*Get! The! Fuck! Out! Of! My! House!*'

"I turned my back on him. I remember thinking I was going to hit him if I didn't leave immediately. If only he had shut up at that point. But no, he needed to get at me. He could not let the shit between us be. If only he had left some things unsaid... But no. He ranted.

"'Get out, you fucking crazy fuck! Get the fuck out of our lives: you and Chris and fucking T. You think you can come hide here and fuck me and fuck my wife, and everybody lives happily ever after? I know what you did! I know how you murdered Uncle George. And I have fucking proof. I am so done with this crazy shit. I can't even begin to explain to other people how fucked up you are!' And on and on. I did not know what the hell he was talking about half the time or why he thought that I murdered Uncle George. He was clearly nuts and in the middle of a huge panic attack."

Ian got up and continued to tell the story as he paced the room.

"At that point, Sheldon put his hands on his knees and took more deep breaths. He looked like shit. Like he couldn't catch his breath. Panic and anger were consuming him.

"In a hoarse, eerie whisper, he said he had spoken with the BC Hydro linesman. He said he had proof that I murdered Uncle George. He was going to call the police and get rid of the fucked-up craziness of our fucking house. He pointed next door.

"I must've said something rude at that point because I was mad. Probably 'fuck you' or something. Then he charged at me. He pushed me hard, and I crashed backward into the counter. He pushed me again. I reached back and got hold of the knife that was right there on the counter.

"It all went red as the anger surged through my body. He kept coming at me like a playground bully. He was hollering, 'Leave, you fuck! Get out of our lives, you murdering son of a fucking bitch.'

"I'd simply had enough. I knew he was about to ruin everything. I slammed the knife into his face. Right between the eyes. It slipped in, down to the handle, in one blow. I was surprised at how easily it went in. Like a hot knife in butter."

Ian stopped pacing.

A smile slowly creeped across his face.

"Oh my God, Catherine, you were right. It feels *so* good to get that off my chest. Legally, I should probably shut up now, but I never liked the guy, to be honest. He looked so surprised at seeing the knife between his eyes. He even squinted to look at it. Then he gurgled, 'What the fuck did you do, you crazy fuck?' He tried to take a deep breath, but instead he turned blue in the face. The blood spurted out of his nose and mouth. His eyes glazed over, and he dropped backward to the floor. I felt nothing for him in that moment. He would have destroyed the world I was protecting.

"His blood is on my hands."

A stunned silence filled the room.

"You have always been Chris's protector, haven't you?" Catherine said quietly.

"Somebody has to look out for the guy."

Catherine's shoulders relaxed, and she smiled kindly at Ian. "One more thing."

"Always one more thing with you, isn't there?"

She nodded. "Did you place the prank call to BC Hydro years ago, when Chris was about to hang himself?"

"Yes. I knew he was about to do something stupid. I figured we might need help."

"Thank you for your honesty, Ian."

There was a shimmer of tears in her eyes as she placed her hand on Ian's arm.

At that moment, Svenson touched his earpiece. "What the fuck?" he said, and stormed out.

Catherine appeared perplexed as she looked at the door. "I'm sorry, Ian. I don't know what that was. Please excuse me."

She grabbed her folder and rushed after Svenson.

20

"What is going on?" Catherine asked.

"You won't fucking believe this." Svenson shook his head.

"What?"

"The cause of death. Sheldon wasn't killed by the stabbing."

"What the fuck?"

"Indeed."

"What *was* the cause, then?"

"I don't know. I just got a call to immediately talk to the pathologist. The message said to stop the interview and confession because the cause of death wasn't the facial stabbing. The pathologist is phoning in. Video conference call. He wants to explain..."

"As he fucking should!" Catherine was pacing the room. "We just cracked this fucking thing wide open, and then they throw the tables over like this?" She tossed her arms in the air. "How could it not be the stabbing? Jesus fucking Christ." Svenson appeared shocked at Catherine's language, and she snapped, "Really? You think I'm always this calm and touchy-feely? No. Fuck. I had it all cracked. We even got the bloody confession, and then..." She slammed the desk with her hand. "Jesus. This had better not fuck it all up."

The computer lit up with the incoming call. Svenson answered, and Catherine pulled another chair closer to sit down.

"Hello, team. Sorry for this. I am Dr. Jonathan Chan, the forensic pathologist. I do have to apologize. I had a junior trainee start out this case, and I only reviewed the case with him today. Obvious injuries have distracted and fooled us all at some point in our career, and in this case my junior fell into that same old trap. To be honest, this was a tough one. Look."

The pathologist displayed a graphic colour photo of the knife sticking out of Sheldon's face.

"Easy to focus on that image, but once you look at the X-ray of the skull," he said, showing the side-view X-ray, "you can see the blade goes from the bridge of the nose, nearly all the way back up to the top of his pharynx, sorry, throat area. But the important issue is that the angle of the tract is slightly downward. The knife did not actually penetrate the cranium portion of the skull. I repeat, the knife did not go into his brain. It caused him to choke on blood, struggle to breathe, and have lots of pain, but the actual stabbing with the knife did not kill him."

Catherine rubbed her forehead. "Okay, Dr. Chan. Thank you. But if the knife didn't kill him, what did? He dropped dead right after he got stabbed. It makes no sense." She was clenching her jaw with frustration.

"Yes. Yes. We will get to it. Very interesting. *Very* interesting. I nearly missed it!" Dr. Chan was very excited.

He produced a picture of the skin. "See these three little dots?"

Catherine and Svenson leaned closer to the screen. "What dots?" Svenson said.

"See? They are easy to miss!" Dr. Chan smiled and brought the picture closer to the webcam. It refocused. "See?"

"Holy mackerel. They're tiny. What are they? Bug bites?" Svenson asked as he squinted.

"That is what my junior thought as well. Since the victim was biking and sleeping outside the day before the incident, it seemed feasible that those could be sandfly bites or something. However, this cluster of dots was on the back of his chest, under his clothes. Therefore, I looked closer and saw there was some bruising through all the layers: from his skin to the muscle, past the ribs into the chest cavity. There was a tiny bruise track."

"Okay. What does it mean?"

"Soon. Soon." Dr. Chan cleared his throat to add some drama. If he had been in the room with them, Catherine would have slapped him already.

"It is important to say, in his defence, that when my junior did the autopsy, he opened the chest and everything looked normal at first glance. But luckily he took lots of pictures, and there was a scout X-ray taken before he opened the chest. We routinely do that to check for bullets or other penetrating objects." Dr. Chan turned to the X-ray monitor behind him. "Can you see this?"

"What are we looking at?" Svenson blurted in irritation.

"The chest X-ray, of course. Look here. The left lung is all black. That means 'not good'—completely collapsed —and the heart is pushed way over onto the right. That is called a tension pneumothorax. He died of a tension pneumothorax!"

"Whoa, whoa, Doc. Go slow. What are you saying?" Svenson scratched his head.

Dr. Chan summarized. "When we put all these facts together, it appears the victim was stabbed three times with a very thin spike, which caused a collapsed lung. That was the cause of death. When there is a puncture of the membrane with a small leaking hole, it creates a one-way valve. When you breath normally, the chest creates negative pressure between the chest wall and the lung, which enables air to flow into the lungs. But if there is a small puncture, air leaks into the space between the lung and the chest wall and builds up there. This is a called a pneumothorax, and if it's small, it is easy to fix. If, however, a pneumothorax increases in size over time, it can become so large that it pushes over the heart and the lung. It can create massive pressure inside the chest cavity until it is impossible to breathe. This is a life-threatening condition. The pressure compresses the heart to prevent it from filling. The heart cannot pump, and you die. With small punctures like these, it builds up slowly until it becomes fatal. Very interesting." Dr. Chan appeared very chuffed.

"If it is so dramatic and obvious, why did you miss it?"

"Um. Problem is, when you open to chest to examine the internal organs, the pressurized air escapes immediately, and everything restores. That is why you must be quiet and listen for escaping air when you open the chest. My junior was listening to music with headphones as he opened the chest. I apologize. He will not make that mistake again. But all is well. The scout X-ray proves the diagnosis."

"What was the murder weapon, then?"

"A very long, thin object. I have only seen this in South African pathological cases. I would guess a sharpened bicycle spoke."

"A bicycle spoke!" Svenson looked at Catherine. "Clever, sneaky fucker..."

Catherine smiled for the first time since the start of the conversation.

Svenson shook his head in amazement. "Wow. Who would have thought?"

"Yep. Very clever." Catherine was scribbling a few notes in her notepad. "Dr. Chan, when would you estimate that the victim was stabbed with this spoke? You said it takes time to develop."

Dr. Chan shrugged. "Difficult to say exactly, but I would estimate from the bruising that it happened about twelve to twenty-four hours before he died."

"Thank you, Dr. Chan," Catherine replied.

"No problem. Sorry for the inconvenience."

They shrugged silently as Dr. Chan ended the video call.

After a stunned silence, Catherine flicked back to some of the earlier pages in her notepad.

"Okay. Okay. I think I get it," she said to herself. "Svenson, can you get the number for the BC Hydro linesman again? I need to confirm something."

21

Catherine twirled her necklace for a while as she sat across from T. On the desk lay a yellow manila envelope.

T winked at Svenson. He was trying hard to appear as flirty and calm as before, but the small bead of sweat on his temple gave away his nerves. He tilted his head sideways to produce a cracking sound from his neck, which he appreciated with an awkward smile.

"Okay, Catherine. You win. I know how this stuff works. I know I am supposed to play it cool and just wait you out, but you know what? I've had enough. I'm tired. I want go home. Did you find the Grindr murderer? I'm sure there are some jealous freaks out there."

She smiled. "Sure are. Interesting side road that you took us on. Thank you. It brought us right back here, though. T... you impress me. People often misjudge you, don't they? Initially, I thought your hints of sophistication and intellect were a superficial cover. Underneath it all, I thought you were weak, scared, and paranoid."

"And now?"

"Oh, now I know you are more clever, calculated, and lethal than I ever suspected."

T lifted his eyebrows, and a cunning smile spread across his face. He looked from Catherine to Svenson and blew him an air kiss. His fingertips showed the slightest tremor.

Catherine continued. "You nearly had us fooled, but eventually we figured out that Sheldon did not die from the stab to his face but from a tension pneumothorax caused by a sneaky stabbing sustained a day before. A stabbing that not even Sheldon was aware of. Very clever. Could have been the perfect murder." She paused.

T tilted his head sideways to show his intrigue.

"It would have been perfect," she continued, "because if Sheldon, a middle-aged emergency doc, suddenly dropped dead at home from an unexplained cardiac arrest, nobody would've ever noticed the three little red dots on his back. His death would have been deemed the result of natural causes. No autopsy required. But all that blood caused by a knife in the face really grabbed our attention, didn't it? Ian really messed that up for you."

T shrugged, nonchalant, and said sarcastically, "Oh, *Ian* was the butcher. Surprise, surprise." T slow-clapped.

Catherine nodded. "Sure was. You probably figured that out long ago."

"It wasn't rocket science. It sure as hell wasn't Chris. Angelique was a maybe, but it would be tough for her to stab a beautiful face like Sheldon's between the eyes. Especially if she still screwed him once in a while. A Grindr suspect was always a stretch. That left an overprotective, impulsive, aggressive assailant... Ian. And you finally got there."

Catherine smiled. "I'm slow and easy. I do not like to assume."

"Hmm."

She pulled the picture from the yellow folder: a colour photo of Sheldon's back. She pointed at the lethal three dots.

"I must confess I underestimated you. Chris said you were the clever one who researched everything and loved to study medicine. That's why you and Sheldon got along. But it takes a certain level of intelligence to do something as calculated as this."

T smiled and looked at the mirror but remained silent.

Catherine pushed the picture away and sat back in her chair. "I spoke with Matthew Sheppard today. Do you recall him?"

T shrugged. "A Grindr date?"

"He's a BC Hydro linesman."

"Yum," T chirped. When Catherine remained expressionless, T sat forward. "Oh, come on! That was funny, wasn't it? Do we have an acute case of humour failure over there?"

Catherine smirked.

T shrugged. "Okay. Whatever. What did Matthew Sheppard, the BC Hydro guy, have to say? I am so fucking intrigued. Not."

"He worked the Vaseux Lake area from the year 2000 till a few months ago. He was there in 2006. He recalled you—"

"Me?"

"Oh, yes. He described you well." Catherine looked at her notepad. "He called you—and I quote—'a soft-spoken, intelligent, gay-appearing, inquisitive teenager with thousands of questions about insulators and high-power lines. A shadow that followed him around with interest.' But when I prompted him about the specific questions you asked, he realized with a shock—no pun intended—that you'd asked how to ground a zip line to prevent electrocution when lightning struck or a high-power line fell on it 'by accident.'" Catherine made air quotes. "It was very curious that in the end, the zip line ended up *not* being grounded at all, even after all that questioning. It was *intentionally* not grounded, to hold the charge..."

T yawned, but Catherine noticed a red blush rise up his neck.

"And then, not too long ago, Matthew received a phone call from someone he initially thought was the police. However, when I asked him today, who do you think was calling him with some blast-from-the-past questions?"

T had an expressionless stare.

"Yep, you guessed it. A guy named Sheldon Peterson. Now why would Sheldon phone him? Because Sheldon was onto you. He was piecing it all together. And I think he told you what he found."

T remained mute.

"Okay. Let me show you something else."

Svenson left the room and returned with a laptop. T winked at him, and Svenson shrugged it off. He opened the laptop and pressed play.

Catherine pointed at the screen. "That's you, T. Old security camera footage found on Sheldon's computer. Take a careful look."

The footage showed a young boy being very busy. His activities included stripping the bark off the base of an old tree that was leaning over the high-power lines.

"It was pretty clever to strip the bark right at the base after sawing the tree trunk at ground level, then patiently waiting for nature to take its course and rot the lake side of the tree trunk. You were careful to saw only the roots on the far side. That way the tree would fall toward the power lines during a big storm, leaving no trace of human interference. Clever, T."

Catherine skipped to the next clip. It showed the same young man digging out the metal base of the zip line and replacing it with a rubber-and-wood base.

"Here you are insulating the zip-line base from the ground, thereby preventing it from being grounded. Now why would anybody do that?" Catherine asked, her voice dripping with sarcasm. "And look there: he's hammering a useless nail into the base of the zip-line post. Incidentally, that was the very same nail that 'accidentally' snagged Mitch's leash. What a coincidence."

The next clip showed a storm raging. Suddenly the big tree fell down and took the high-power lines with it. The lines landed on the zip line, sending arcs and sparks flying.

A blurry image appeared of someone running out in the rain with a small dog and tying the leash to the nail.

"Poor little Mitch," Catherine whispered softly.

The image of Uncle George running out in the storm appeared on screen. He grabbed Mitch. A spectacular arc blazed across the screen as Uncle George grabbed onto the zip-line post and grounded the 200,000-volt charge trapped in the zip line.

T stared at the screen as if in a trance.

"Poor little Mitch," Catherine repeated with true empathy in her voice.

Tears ran across T's face. "Poor little Mitch," he sobbed.

"Why did you kill Mitch?" Catherine asked softly.

"I didn't mean to! Fuck. I didn't expect Uncle George would grab Mitch *before* he grabbed the zip-line post. He was an old fuck. I thought he would grab the post first, to have something to hold onto as he leaned down to pick up Mitch!"

As the words hung in the air, T's face ashened. "I said that out loud, didn't I?"

Catherine leaned back in her chair and slowly put down her pen. She looked up at the video camera to confirm that the red light was flashing.

T sat back. He placed his hands behind his head. A wry smile bloomed across his face. He nodded at Catherine. "Well done, Catherine. Respect. You won."

Catherine acknowledged the praise with a slight nod. "I suspected Mitch might be your blind spot."

She pulled an evidence bag out her handbag on the floor. A cell phone.

"Sheldon's phone. The compilation of clips I played to you was in a drop box account—and you know what? Sheldon accessed that account, from this phone, on Wednesday... when he was bikepacking with you. The video viewings are date stamped for when you two were on the bike trip. That is very compelling evidence."

She leaned down and retrieved a second bag from the floor. In the bag were two spare bicycle spokes.

"On your last bikepacking trip, when you raced the BC Epic 1000 from Merritt to Fernie, you blogged about it. In the blog, there is a beautifully clear picture of all the gear you rode with... and look over here."

She pulled a picture from the yellow envelope and tapped it. "Look! You wrote in the blog, 'I always ride with at least three spare bicycle spokes.' And here's the picture of them."

She touched the evidence bag with the spokes in it. "One, two... I wonder what happened to number three?"

"All circumstantial," T said.

"Maybe. But there's opportunity and motive. I think a jury will find the math as easy as"—she made the words rhyme—"one, two, three. Checkmate, T."

She pushed the evidence to the side and looked straight at T. "You don't have to say anything further at this point. We have it on tape that you killed Uncle George. You admitted to it. We also know that Sheldon knew. We know he showed you the evidence on the bike trip by looking at the drop box download time stamp. We know one spoke is missing from your gear, and we know he died the next day after being stabbed by a bicycle spoke. It would not be a stretch for a jury to conclude that you quietly stabbed him three times during the night on your bike trip and patiently waited for the pneumothorax to develop thereafter. I think we have you: lock, stock, and barrel."

T clapped slowly. He looked at the camera. Red light flashing.

"Come on, T. You know we've got you on this. Why don't you simply get this off your chest? I know you want tell us why. What did Sheldon want? Was he threatening to go to the police?"

T looked at the mirror for a moment and said, "Ah, fuck it. Fucking Sheldon. I thought he was the king of this casual love stuff. Why the fuck did he have to fall in love with me? He had played these games all his life. Why did he have to lose the plot like that? Geez. He wanted to blackmail me with Uncle George's death to force me to run away with him. And leave Angelique. What sort of guy runs away from his pregnant wife? Sure, he wasn't into Angelique—or any woman—anymore, but what about Chris and Angelique and the baby? Fuck. I told him to grow a pair. I told him not to rock the boat. I told him Chris needed Angelique and vice versa.

"I don't think he ever understood the bond between me, Chris, and Ian. We fitted perfectly. What an arrogant narcissist he was, thinking I'd break that up for him. That I'd ruin it all to be with him. But the Uncle George thing would have sunk me, and he was threatening to take it to the police. So while he slept like a baby after we'd finished off a bottle of Fireball, I went looking for my spare bicycle spokes.

"I'd read about bicycle spoke stabbings long before that night. I thought it was cool. I made a mental note. It would be the perfect murder weapon if one were so inclined. You never know when you might need knowledge like that.

"The spare spoke came in handy."

22

Shattered Mirror

C hris was smiling. It was the first time since the murder that T and Ian had joined him in the interrogation room.

He looked down at his hands, wondering how it all came to be.

T spoke. "Sorry, Chris."

"I thought I was the one that killed him," Ian said in surprise. "Now I hear it was actually you, T. Why?"

T shrugged. "Same reason you stabbed him. He was going to ruin it all. He wanted to run away. Didn't want women in his life anymore, and certainly no kids. I knew that wouldn't sit right with you, Chris."

Chris nodded. "The two of you have always looked out for me."

"Well, we all need each other in some way," Ian said.

"Too bad you dragged me in here, though. You really fucked up things up, Ian," T grumbled.

"*I* fucked it up? I tried to stop Sheldon. It got out of hand."

"You're such an impulsive idiot. It was perfect. Perfect! Nobody would have known... But no. Ian had to pour blood all over it and shine a freaking spotlight on it. Admit it: you fucked it up."

"Maybe, but it was you who killed Uncle George. That's what Sheldon was talking about! He was blaming me. But it was you, wasn't it?"

"What?" Chris said in shock. "T? Did you kill Uncle George and Mitch? I thought it was the lightning! You killed Mitch?"

"We all know Uncle George needed to die. He was the Thin Man."

"But you killed Mitch..." Chris burst into tears.

Ian screamed at the top of his voice. "Come on! Tell us! Why did you fucking kill Mitch?" He grabbed the chair and threw it across the room in frustration. It shattered the one-way mirror.

As the glass fell to the floor, Chris looked up to see Catherine standing in the observation room behind it. She was hugging Angelique, who was wailing with tears.

"Oh my God. I never knew," Angelique cried.

Chris looked over at her, and they stared at each other. Stunned.

"Who the fuck *are* you, Chris?" Angelique cried. "And who the fuck are T and Ian?"

Chris, T, and Ian looked at the pieces of shattered mirror on the floor as they knelt down to clean up the mess. As they gathered the shards together, some pieces reflected Chris, some reflected Ian, and others reflected T.

But when all the pieces were gathered, they reflected only *one* face.

. . .

SVENSON ENTERED the room and said, "Christian Miller, you are under arrest for the murder of Dr. Sheldon Peterson. You have the right to remain silent. Anything you say can and will be used against you in a court of law."

Only one person had ever called Chris by his full name. He heard his mom's voice echo from the back door in the kitchen, a time long before the Thin Man visited him the first time:

"Chris-T-Ian! Come on home—dinner is ready!"

Christian turned his back and Svenson handcuffed him. As he walked out toward the cells, he watched Angelique being consoled by Catherine. All he saw was her head bobbing slightly as she cried.

"Hush," Catherine said as she held Angelique. "It'll all be okay. He'll get help. That's why Svenson called me in at the start."

Angelique pulled back and looked at Catherine with a perplexed expression.

"I am not a police investigator in the normal sense," Catherine said in explanation. "I am a forensic psychologist. I assist the police."

"What is going on?"

"Chris has led a life of extreme stress, abuse, and isolation. As a defence mechanism against this trauma, he developed dissociative identity disorder. It is a rare and very controversial condition, but I believe that true cases like Chris's need to be studied. He needs help. I was called in to document the disorder and determine whether this was a real case or if he was faking it. I am convinced Chris's is a true case. The documentation pertaining to this investigation will help him, because the Chris you know truly did not intend to harm. However, his alter identities, T and Ian, fulfill other aspects of his psyche. Ian was the aggressor with whom you did interact on occasion. The episodes of violent sex and, I think, your first sexual experience..."

Angelique nodded and mumbled, "Oh my God, I knew he was different at times!"

"And T was Chris's homosexual identity."

"But it is all still Chris's body. How could you tell them apart?"

Catherine smiled. "I have been doing this for a while. Human identity is not defined only by what we look like but also by our personalities, behaviours, and mannerisms. Chris is sensitive, cries easily, wrings his hands or has tremors, looks nervous or jumpy, and he sits on the edge of his chair.

"The moment Ian appeared, he was up out of the chair: aggressive, confrontational, and meaner—even condescending and intolerant.

"And T has a slightly different tone of voice and enunciation. He is calmer, more confident, well-spoken. I don't know if you were aware, but Sheldon and T were seeing each other. However, things changed when Sheldon fell in love with the strong, silent, intelligent T. Sheldon would come up to the house and ask whether 'T was in?' He was asking for that identity to come forward."

"Oh my God. Sheldon knew about this?"

"Oh, yes. And he used it. He wanted T to become dominant and Chris's persona to be suppressed. And Sheldon had other, more devious plans. He was hoping to elope with T. But I don't want to upset you further."

"Obviously T didn't go for that. He stayed loyal to Chris... and me?"

Catherine nodded her head with a wry smile. "Blood is always thicker than water. Sheldon overplayed his hand. In fact, he had no clue what he was tampering with, and when he threatened one identity, he threatened them all. As different as they are, they are always one."

Angelique looked down at her laced fingers as the tears made her vision shimmer. "Always one, with blood on his hands..."

ACKNOWLEDGEMENTS

My writing would have never seen the light of day without the feedback, support, and encouragement I received from my friends and family. Alan and Tamara Vukusic, Diana Hauser, and Melinda Uys were instrumental with their encouragement and assistance from the beginning. Thank you to Marina van Zyl, Ellen Jacobson, and all others who have read the drafts and guided me to the final product through your candid commentary. It is said, "It takes a village to raise a child." Completing a novel is like nurturing a child to adulthood. I thank you all.

Amanda Bidnall, your editing for *Blood on His Hands* truly transformed the mystery to its knife's-edge conclusion! Thank you so much for your patience and guidance.

Crystal Stranaghan, your team at Crystal Clear Solutions made this happen from the start! I cannot thank you enough for everything you have orchestrated over the years. You are simply magnificent.

Stephanie Candiago, thank you for the wonderful

layout for *Blood on His Hands* and for getting this book published in all formats.

Constance Mears, thanks for the strikingly spectacular cover and presentation.

As the COVID-19 pandemic rages on, I want to thank all the staff in all emergency rooms in the world for the tremendous work you do night and day, saving the lives of others while putting your own at risk. Many of the battles you fight go unseen. Many of sacrifices you make go unnoticed. I am proud to be your colleague and pay tribute to your legacy.

ABOUT THE AUTHOR

HENK MUNI

I was born in South Africa and became an emergency physician during the violent era of my birth land's transformation from the ashes of apartheid to a new rainbow nation. In the South African trauma rooms, I witnessed humans' ability to inflict misery and pain upon each other, and I hoped to expose a bit of that brutal world in my writing.

I self-published my first novel, *See-Saw*, a medical psychological thriller, and then moved towards my roots with my second novel, *Against the Wall*.

My third book, *Blood on His Hands*, investigates the murder of a successful emergency physician in a quiet lakeside community, as the layers of complexity behind a seemingly normal life are peeled away.

On our uncertain journey through life, our biggest challenges quite often blindside us. During those times, we often seek answers from our peers, friends, elders, and teachers. Sometimes we turn to religion or the written word. We share these questions with others to enlighten our own perspectives. As a qualified emergency physician, I am privileged to observe the world from a different viewpoint. Daily, I witness people having the worst—and, on occasion, the best—days of their lives. I hope to illuminate these crucial and sometimes dark moments in my search for clarity and truth. I believe that experiencing life, not only through your own senses but also through the perceptions of your fellow voyagers, will completely transform your perspective.

Currently, I am a proud Canadian from beautiful British Columbia.

OTHER TITLES BY HENK MUNI

When Dr. Michael Clarke plummets to his death, his colleague and best friend Peter is left reeling. What could account for his charismatic friend's fatal decision?

As Peter searches the past for answers, he must reckon with their complicated history. From classmates in med school to blood brothers and romantic rivals, from the sultry beaches of Cape Town to the bitter cold of Western Canada, their relationship has see-sawed wildly between love and competition. Was their unresolved quarrel over the beautiful Sandra the tipping point?

Or is one of these men harboring a much darker secret?

AVAILABLE NOW ON AMAZON

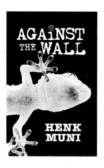

1981. Pretoria: heartland of the Afrikaner. As the violence of the armed struggle against apartheid is threatening to overwhelm South Africa, eight-year-old Pieter Pretorius tries to unravel the secrets within his own household, which his nationalist, rugby-loving father rules with an iron fist. Thom Isaacs is a Jewish police constable whose moral awakening and disgust with the systemic and racial violence of his government threatens to out him among his fellow officers as a "lefty" and a traitor. In one week, Pieter and Thom will cross paths in a bloody confrontation that sees Pieter staring down the barrel of a gun and Thom racing to save another victim from the spiraling chaos that is tearing their homeland apart.

AVAILABLE NOW ON AMAZON